A JANUARY STUDIOS NOVELLA

A Little Bit Inspired

DEDICATION

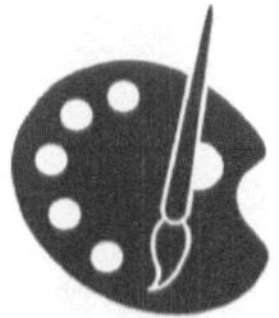

You're important. You're loved. You're enough.
This novella is for you.

Content Warning

Thank you for picking up Tyler and Lucy's story. Before reading, I want to let you know there are panic attacks on page. Everyone's experience is different; this is mine.

1
LUCY

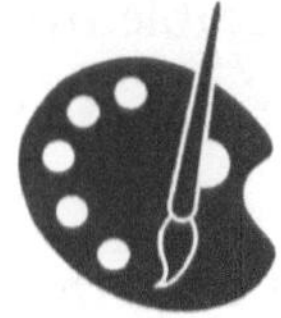

I DON'T KNOW WHY I thought wearing this damn dress was a good idea. It's too tight. And short. Definitely too short.

But what else does one wear to a celebrity's 30th birthday party? One where their best friend practically begged (asked nicely) for them to attend?

The curls staying in my hair even though I've been running around the diner for the past few hours is a plus. Looking in the mirror, I touch up the almost-purple circles under my eyes with a small amount of concealer and call it good. It's dark in the venue, right? Is anyone going to be looking at me close enough to tell that I haven't slept much this past week?

I've been so busy. Not only have I been serving at Dave's Diner almost every evening for the last six years, but lately I'm working overtime at the art studio to perfect my paintings for a very important showcase this fall. It's time for a change.

Because I'm always on the night shift with my best friend and roommate, Cassie, we are perpetually exhausted. During the day, I'm working on my art, painting, or *trying* to paint as of late. My ultimate goal is to paint full-time, and I may have a chance to do that soon, but for now I'm stuck delivering burgers and pasta until early hours of the morning.

A knock on the bathroom door shakes me from my thoughts, which is impeccable timing because once I start thinking about the showcase, I can't stop myself from spiraling.

"Just a minute!" I holler to the mystery person, who is no doubt a crew member from January Studios, one of Los Angeles' top movie studios, which is right across the street. If I didn't have to work tonight, I'd *maybe* feel better about spending time with nearly 100 people in a crowded nightclub. That's too many people for one night when I've already spent the better half of today wearing a fake smile to please strangers.

I allow myself a final look in the mirror, then open the door to shimmy past the patron. I keep my head down to avoid unwarranted conversations as I sneak through the dining room and out the front door.

The weather in LA is hot, as always, and I speed-walk to my car to avoid the little makeup I put on from melting off.

I also make sure to fire off a text to Cassie to let her know I'm on my way. As soon as I press send, my phone vibrates. *Ugh.* I do not need this tonight.

"What?" I answer, buckling my seatbelt and starting the car, making sure to put the air on full blast.

"Are you avoiding me?" the bane of my existence asks.

"I did tell you to stop calling me, didn't I?" Why did I answer the phone again? Cassie would tell me to block Jake's number for what he did to me and she barely knows anything about him.

"Baby, I told you it didn't mean anything."

"It didn't—" I sigh, loud enough to ensure Jake hears it. "It doesn't matter. Stop calling me."

Jake and I were together for six months. Then he cheated on me with another artist at my studio. Someone who I would have considered a friend, which can be hard to come by when you're in a field that breeds and encourages competition. I should have known something was going on when Kelly stopped being able to paint with me and Jake was all of a sudden *busy* on the same nights. We broke up a few weeks ago.

Fucker.

I hang up as he talks, not wanting to listen to whatever he has to say. It's just another bullet point to add to my *Reasons Lucy Doesn't Date* list.

By the time I pull up to Moonlight Club I have a change of heart and I'm ready to dance, and drink, and have some fun for once. Tonight is for me, even if that means conversing with more strangers. No painting, no stressing out about the showcase that will impact my entire art career, no fuckboys. Emphasis on the last one.

There are *a lot* of people outside the club. Photographers, journalists, random fans—and what do I do? I, regrettably, pull the car up to the valet, because I'm not sure what another option would be. Being somewhere other than my art studio, home, or the diner feels as foreign as learning a new language for the first time. Even though I grew up in California and have lived in LA for the past six years, I have never been to an event like this. I've never crossed paths with people who can afford an event like this.

"Miss, miss, look here," a photographer shouts as soon as I step out of my car.

I look and wave, like an idiot, then hurry toward the door. More people shout my way, but I pretend to not hear them and keep walking. Being on gossip sites is not on my bucket list.

The darkness of the club is a little jarring at first, but as my eyes adjust, I notice the soft glow of red lights to highlight various parts of the venue. Loud music blares to my right as I search for Cassie through the various groups of people.

It's not until I scan the room for the third time that I see Cassie waving to me from the dance floor surrounded by very, *very* handsome men. She's wearing black from head to toe, which is probably why I couldn't see her. If it wasn't for her brown hair and bright red lip, she'd blend into her surroundings.

"Damn, Luce," Cassie says as I approach, and I humor her by spinning in a circle.

"Oh, this thing?" I glance down at my dress, deciding to own that I look hot as fuck tonight. "Dress to impress, right?" I glance back up and pull Cassie into a hug.

When I finally let her go, I look around to see two guys staring my way. I know Emmett from serving him at the diner when he first met Cassie a few weeks ago, but I'm not sure who his friend is.

I reintroduce myself to Emmett, a.k.a. the celebrity celebrating his birthday. "Hi, I'm Lucy, the best friend, if you don't remember me from a few weeks ago at the diner."

"How could I forget? I'm Emmett, the uh..." *Dude that has it bad for my best friend?* "This is Tyler," he says instead, choosing to default to the easier thing to voice.

I direct my attention to the extremely tall and attractive man Emmett's pointing to. Tyler runs a hand through his dirty blond hair, smiling my way as the pieces fall back to either side of his face. His hair, parted down the middle, isn't wavy, but it's not straight either—there's enough texture that the length shapes his face perfectly. When he gets close enough, the light from the surrounding spotlights showcase golden flecks in his dark green eyes, and I'm swooning internally.

And also wishing Cassie showed me a picture of this man before this evening because *hot damn*, it's hard to tear my eyes away from his gaze.

I do not need another bullet point to add to my list, and by the way nearby females are looking his way, I can already predict being around Tyler would add more than one.

"Join me for a drink?" I blurt out anyway, and he nods immediately. When I turn to face Cassie, she's looking my way with a smile. Tonight means a lot to her, and although she invited me here, I know she wants to spend time alone with Emmett.

Tyler grabs my hand, and I let him. Together, we weave through clumps of people as they sway to the beat. I manage to dodge a few couples that aren't paying attention, and also manage to not shove them back.

That's a win for me.

When we reach the bar, Tyler keeps walking around the edge until we are on the far side, farthest away from any speaker.

He leans into my bubble to whisper in my ear. "It'll be quieter on this end."

It's at this moment that I question my decisions to both ask Tyler to grab a drink and to follow him to a dark corner. Is it smart to be sitting here with a man I just met? Maybe not, but let's just assume fate is at work tonight and we were meant to meet. I'd rather not upset the universe and her signs. Reminder: I'm here to have a drink, have some fun, do this for me. Sitting with Tyler might go against my "no fuckboys" rule, but rules are meant to bend, right? At least, that's what I'm telling myself as I sit here and stare at the handsome man in front of me as his muscles flex and he fidgets with the menu. Besides, I don't want to be a third wheel to Cassie and her man, so this seems like the safest option since I know literally no one else in this room.

"What are you drinking tonight?" Tyler asks.

"Um." Good question. "Just club soda is fine, with lime."

He nods and turns to the bartender, shouting our order even though he doesn't need to. Tyler orders himself the same thing but with lemon.

"I want to know something." Tyler turns to me and leans his elbow on the bar, catching his head with a hand.

I have a feeling I know where this is going.

"What?" I cross my right leg over my left and mimic his position to lean into the bar.

"What is it like to be the most gorgeous person in this room?"

I swear to God his eyes sparkle and as he smirks, dimples form.

And what do I do? I laugh. I laugh for a solid three minutes. I laugh so hard that I have to cover my mouth to avoid having a full on giggle attack because that is not what I expected.

"And here I was thinking you were the quiet one," I finally manage to say after taking a long drink.

"Ha, not at all. But you *could* think I'm the sexy one," Tyler muses.

"I could," I say. "Although, I think the guy behind you might take that spot."

"The—who—" Tyler whips his head around to face the wall. There is no guy. Just a lot of bricks. He palms his chin, turning back to me with a sly smile.

"You walked into that one." I shrug.

"I like you, Lucy." Tyler says it so easily that I'm taken aback.

What is there to like? I can't keep a relationship to save my life, I can't paint matching pieces for the showcase. My inspiration is nowhere to be seen, and because of that, my life is being held together by strings.

The pressure of the showcase has stunted any inspiration I had. In my decade of painting, from a teenager throwing random colors on a canvas to a student finding their niche in the industry, I've always had a vision of what I wanted to paint. And even if it took me a few days, a week at most, I'd be able to step back and see it come to life.

But right now? For the showcase that could change my career? My mind is blank, and it's been like this for months. Demonstrate my art, get a permanent spot in the gallery. That is what's at stake. And me being me (overly confident and always thinking without speaking), I decided to commit to a three-piece abstract painting. I could have committed a few separate works, or used one from a previous showcase, but I knew I had to go all out if I wanted *this* to be the showcase that opens doors.

Lucky me, right? Tonight is exactly what I need. A reset, maybe, to jog some motivation or inspiration to figure out what I want to paint.

"I suppose you're alright."

"Just alright?" Tyler throws a hand to his chest. "That hurts, pretty girl."

A nickname, already. My heart stutters, once, twice, three times. My hands are clammy, and it's not from the condensation of the drink. The attention that Tyler is giving me is what I thought I wanted after talking with Jake earlier, but I'm finding that my heart is still fragile.

He doesn't talk for the next few minutes, just twists in his chair to stare at the dance floor.

So I do the same.

2
TYLER

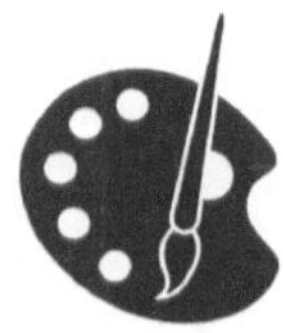

The nickname for Lucy rolls off my tongue without me thinking about it. One glance at her, a single conversation, and I'm trying harder than I have with any girl I've seen over the past year.

That's the thing I can't wrap my head around. I've hardly spoken to her, yet I find myself stumbling over my own thoughts, and that never happens. She didn't exactly say it, but I *am* the loud one. I never have an issue flirting with women; it's what I'm good at.

I've been planning tonight's party for Emmett for the past month with two of our other best friends, Lane and Max. Out of our group, I'm the one that always has a different woman hanging off my arm. I never repeat, never call them back, never give them a chance to fall for me.

But Lucy...

There's something intriguing about her that has me wanting to beg her to talk to me all night.

Talk.

Fuck.

That's how I know I have it bad within the first hour of knowing her. Her tight fucking dress, so damn short I can tell that she's either wearing a thong or no underwear at all. That paired with the loose auburn curls floating around her shoulders, and she has me in a chokehold.

Yeah, I'd like to see what kind of fun we could get into, but there's something holding me back from making my typical move to end the night early and go back to my place.

Maybe it's because it's Emmett's birthday party.

Maybe it's because this is Cassie's best friend and Cassie and Emmett have something going on.

Or maybe it's because she gives off a different vibe; one that has me hesitating.

I should wave a white flag, walk away from the conversation, but I don't.

"Want to move to the booth? I see that Cassie and Emmett are cozied up." I lean over to ask in her ear.

Her eyes drop from mine to the goosebumps that line her arm, then back up to my face. She tucks her bottom lip and I watch as she slowly releases it. She's going to be trouble, I already know it.

"We can do that," Lucy says after giving herself a moment to think it over.

I stand from the bar and walk toward the booth, sliding in first before Lucy slides in after me.

"Well, helloooo lovebirds," I yell over the music. Emmett glances at Cassie, and I know what he's thinking without having to say it.

"What have you two been up to?" Emmett asks.

Play the part.

I throw my arm around Lucy but regret it when she tenses under me. "Oh, you know, little bit of this, little bit of that."

"We got a drink." Lucy deadpans while she grabs my hand and moves my arm, which I saw coming a mile away.

When I catch her gaze, there's an emotion on her face that I'm not used to. It has a hint of yearning, but it's cautious. Like she wants to give in, but she's not going to let herself.

Cassie and Emmett move to go dance, but before they leave, Cassie stops to speak to Lucy.

"Just let me know when you plan on leaving," is the last thing I hear Lucy say before Cassie disappears through the crowd with Emmett.

I pinch her side and she yelps.

"What was that?" Her hand moves to her side, to pretend that it hurts, but based on the upward curve of her lips, I know it doesn't.

"Just wanted to make sure this wasn't a dream." I shrug, my flirtation officially turned up to an eight. I still have room to go before the night is over.

"You're supposed to pinch yourself," she says, her brows furrowing.

"Is that what I'm supposed to do? I wonder what else you can teach me," I tease, leaning an elbow on the table.

She laughs, sending a flutter through my body. It's such an unfamiliar feeling that I'm on the fence if I want to get her to do it again or if I want to harden my armor.

"Tyler." Lucy copies my position, leaning her elbow on the table to stare at me.

"Lucy," I mimic.

With the way we are sitting in the booth, it's like we're in our own little world. The dark lights, the slow music, the lack of people around us even though the venue is packed, and the way we are sitting make it *feel* like a dream.

A dream that shouldn't be.

My cheeks hurt from the smile I can't seem to get rid of.

"Tyler." Lucy says my name again, and I swear to God if she says it one more time, I'm going to grab her chin and pull her lips to mine.

"Go on a date with me," I whisper.

"What?" She leans closer, stopping when she's only a few inches from me. I wonder if I try to touch her if she'll push me away again.

I reach out to bring my free hand to her thigh and lean in until I'm hovering next to her face.

"I said, go on a date with me."

She doesn't move my hand, not yet, and neither do I.

I don't shift back either, leaving my face next to hers, feeling her breath hot against me.

"I don't go on dates," she says.

"I don't go on dates either."

"Then—," she takes a breath, shakes her head, glances at my hand on her leg then back to me, "but I *really* don't go on dates."

"And I really don't go on dates either." I squeeze, not too hard, enough to hopefully send some secret signal. Some signal I don't even fully know or understand yet.

"I'm not looking for anything at the moment."

"Maybe I'm not looking for anything at the moment either," I say with a shrug.

"Are you going to repeat everything I say, Tyler? If so, I don't see this ever working."

"No, pretty girl. Because I do see this working." The name for her just rolls off the tip of my tongue.

"Oh, you do?" Lucy shifts in her seat, taking her elbow off the table and leaning back into the cushion. In doing so, my hand shifts higher on her thigh, but still, she doesn't move it.

That's got to mean something, right? I've never been great at reading others, probably because I didn't grow up with a lot of people around to begin with. From a young age, I had to learn how to be me, but better. I always had to fight for myself but make sure I kept to myself. Keep a low profile, don't ask for help, tomorrow's a new day. That's what I lived by until I moved to my own place and stopped talking to my mom.

"Mhm, I do. Haven't you figured out that I'm fairly confident about everything by now?" I ask.

She laughs and says, "Tyler, I just met you."

"And it feels like we've known each other forever, I know. I feel it too." I squeeze her leg once more as her cheeks reach a deeper shade of red, matching the interior of the venue. "But remind me again what you do for a living?"

Lucy glances to the left and back at me, all while wearing a sly smirk. "Oh, you don't know that about me? I got the feeling you kinda knew everything."

It's my turn to laugh now, and I pull back my hand from her leg to catch my head as I lean back in the seat. "She's sexy *and* funny? Shit." I shake my head in disbelief and remind myself to not mess this up.

"I'm a woman of many talents, one of which is painting art for a living," she says and grabs her drink from the table to take a sip.

"An artist."

"An artist." She nods. "But unfortunately if I can't find the right inspiration for my current piece, I don't know what will happen..." Lucy trails off, her stare returning to her legs.

"Let me help," I blurt before I know what I'm saying.

She lifts her eyes, and even though there is curiosity in her gaze, she's hesitant. And I don't blame her. She doesn't know me. Why should she trust a word I say? And also, her best friend, who is our connection, hardly knows me, so I'm a stranger at best.

"What do you know about a—"

"Creating art is kind of like cooking, right?" I say, scrambling to find reasons to convince her to spend time with me. "You have a vision in mind, you have the ingredients you need… and it's all about ensuring that everything comes together in the right way to create the perfect dish. Or in your case, a painting."

"You cook?" She lifts a brow, trying to change the subject.

"If you agree to go on a date with me, maybe you'll find out."

"I—"

Cassie returns to the booth with a huff, distracting Lucy from finishing her sentence. We both turn to face her.

"Where's Emmett?" I ask, and not even five seconds later, he comes to the table and slides in next to Cassie.

"I thought I told you to mingle." Cassie directs her attention to Emmett.

"I thought I said this isn't over," Emmett replies, his eyes remaining on Cassie as if it was their turn to be in their own little world. Even though this is Emmett's party, I'm fairly certain that he only wants to hang out with Cassie. I wouldn't be surprised if they left early.

Cassie shifts her entire body to Emmett and they just stare at each other, their sexual tension washing over the entire table reminding me that Lucy is sitting next to me.

I glance in her direction to find her already looking at me, and when I smirk to let her know she's been caught, she curls her lips inward between her teeth. Her eyes venture back to the other side of the booth.

"I think I'm going to leave," Emmett says. I called it.

I nod to let him know that he can do what he wants. We have the party covered. He and Cassie talk for only a moment more before they say goodbye and head off for the evening.

"So…" I lean toward Lucy and whisper in her ear. She whips around to face me, her mouth nearly crashing with mine.

"Oh my God, Tyler," she says, her lips merely inches from mine.

"You know what I'm thinking right now?"

Lucy glances at my mouth as I trace my bottom lip with my tongue. Her eyes darken as they meet mine and she takes a deep breath before whispering, "What?"

If there was a time to shoot my shot, that time is now. *Here goes nothing*.

"You look like a great kisser, and I'm wondering if you'll let me see if I'm right."

Her lips begin to curl up in a smile as she ponders how to respond. My flirtation has officially hit the max and I'm hoping, *hoping*, she will say yes to a date. I need to know what it's like to take Lucy out. I don't know why, but deep down, I feel like if I don't then I'll regret it for the rest of my life.

She shrugs. "There's one way to find out."

3

LUCY

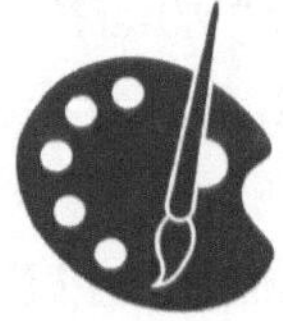

Tyler looks at me, surprise apparent on his face, as I say the words he wasn't expecting to hear. After rejecting his requests for a date, I know he expected me to say no, to push him away.

And I think if this was ten minutes ago, I would have.

But then I saw Cassie and the way that Emmett was looking at her. It's the same way Tyler is looking at me right now. His eyes full of lust, of pure intentions, of hope. They circle my face, waiting for me to back away, to tell him I was kidding.

Instead, I lean forward the final inch and press my lips to his.

Tyler lets out a moan, and his hand shifts to the back of my neck. Our soft kiss begins to quicken, shifting to echo our personalities. His free hand finds my waist, and he pulls me toward him as his head tilts to the side.

I let him drag me until I'm sitting on his lap, nestled between him and the table.

"Fuck," he grumbles in between kisses. "*Lucy*."

We don't let up. Our tongues dance. His grip tightens around my hips before it trails to my back to pull me closer, leaving no room between us. His hand tugs on my hair, and because of that, I start to grind on his lap, needing more.

My body reacts on its own accord. My hands rest on his shoulders to give me something to hold on to as I move along with the beat of my heart.

"Wait," Tyler says. He pulls back from me and rests his forehead on mine. His breathing is ragged and taxed from the short make out session.

"How was that?" I ask.

"How was *that*?" Tyler repeats, pulling back to look at me. His hand comes to my face to tuck a piece of hair behind my ear. "Fucking perfect. And God if I don't want to fuck you right now..."

"Do you always say what's on your mind?" I ask, knowing I should be wary of how forward he is, but him being blunt is actually what's drawing me in. I *like* that he blurts out whatever is on his mind, that I know what he's thinking at any given moment. It's refreshing to feel wanted, especially after only meeting him tonight.

He's different from Jake, or any previous guy I've dated. Instead of actually communicating with words, I've been texted memes and ghosted. Is it too much to ask for a guy to pay attention to you, text you "good morning" every day, and support you while you chase your dream? Apparently so. That's why it's already different with Tyler. In the hour that

I've known him, he's shown more interest than anyone before showed over months.

He chuckles and says, "Not usually. For some reason my brain can't seem to understand that I'm trying *really* hard to impress you tonight and not fuck this up."

I scoot off his lap, back onto the booth cushion. We *are* still at a club with many, many individuals and even though the lights are low, I don't want to draw extra attention.

"I'm thinking about changing my answer to an earlier question you asked, if you, uhh, wanted to ask it again," I say. My belly flutters at the way he's looking at me.

"Go on a date with me?" He smiles wide, and I swear that this is what love at first sight feels like.

My chest is tight with anticipation. My legs feel like jello even though I'm sitting down. I can't stop my eyes from grazing over his. And my stomach won't stop doing flip after flip after flip.

"That's not—" I start to say, and his smile drops. His eyes widen and he's about to say something, but I interrupt him. "I'm kidding. Yes, I will go on a date with you, Tyler."

"Fuck, pretty girl, you nearly gave me a heart attack."

Tyler playfully shoves my shoulder and we both laugh.

"I had to, I'm sorry." I shrug.

"You're just trying to rile me up," he suggests.

"I already did that..." I drawl, dragging my gaze down his body.

"Mm, yeah, I suppose you did," he agrees. Tyler reaches behind him and takes his phone out of his pocket. "I'll text you details?"

"Sure." I smile and type in my name and number and hand it back to him.

"Okay, cool," Tyler says. His voice quivers slightly, I can tell he's trying to be chill about this, even though the smile on his face and the blushing on his cheeks give him away. And it's cute, really cute, to see him happy about something as simple as my phone number and going on a date with him.

"Walk me out?" I ask as I loop my bag around my shoulder.

He nods, so I slip out of the booth and wait for him to stand next to me.

"Let me tell the valet to bring your car around the back. The door is over there," he points to the other side of the room and is gone the moment I hand him my ticket.

I'm grateful to not have to go out the front door. The last thing I feel like doing is having people holler at me again and think that I'm someone notable.

Weaving through the crowd, I locate the door and push through to the warm night air to find Tyler somehow already on the other side with my car.

"Thank you," I say as I approach.

"I figured you might not want the cameras in your face."

I chuckle. "Not particularly, no."

I round the front of the car and stop by the driver-side door. Tyler follows me, breathing life into the butterflies in my stomach. Actually, it's more like a tornado, or a swarm of bees, or a tsunami wave.

"Thank you, also, for tonight, for keeping me company. I had fun." I smile.

"Oh yeah?" He takes one, two, three steps toward me, inching me closer to the car until my back hits the hard surface. He brings a hand to either side of me and rests them on the vehicle, pinning me between.

My breath is heavy, and deep down I know that falling into something else so soon is bad. It's bad, right? I shouldn't want to be with someone new. I shouldn't want to spend time with anyone. I *need* to focus on my art. If I don't, I'll be stuck at the diner waiting for another opportunity to showcase my art.

But I can't deny the immediate feelings I have for Tyler. The way he looks at me like I'm the only woman who has made him fall to his knees, that I'm the one he's been waiting for, wishing for.

I tilt my chin up, and he follows my lead by leaning in again.

Slow and steady, he kisses me. My hands wrap around his waist and I pull him into me, needing to feel his body against mine. The pull between us is too great to ignore, and part of me wonders if this is just *him*, if he's this way with everyone. That all women are drawn to him because of the way he looks and talks to them.

But then the other part of me thinks it can't be, not with the way he's touching me, and the way he's been chasing me all night.

"God, I *really* like you," he whispers once we finally end our kiss.

"I like you too," I whisper back.

He's smiling, and I don't have to look at his mouth to know that. I can tell from the way he releases a breath and the way his shoulders sag just a little bit in relief.

"So, I'll text you," he says.

"And I'll be waiting."

Tyler pushes off the car and takes a step back.

"Great, um, drive home safe, okay?" He threads a hand through his hair.

"I will."

Tyler steps toward me again and leans to press a kiss on my cheek. "See you soon, pretty girl."

He walks away, and as I get into my car and drive home, I'm still smiling as I play back the memories of tonight.

4

TYLER

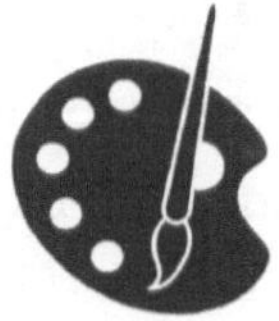

Ten minutes passed until I couldn't wait any longer to send Lucy a text.

How else was she going to tell me she made it home? That's what I'm telling myself, anyway.

I told her I liked her and she said it back.

My life suddenly feels like a movie, and I'm not sure how I feel about it. Even with it being the next morning, I find my thoughts replaying every minor detail from last night: the smiles, the touches, the *kisses*. Plural.

I lead catering at January Studios, so I'm used to seeing people pretend for a living when filming scenes. And because of that, I know where to look to find body language that may tell me when someone is putting on an act, or saying something just because they think it's what I want to hear.

All night I tried to spot it on Lucy, that look or the change in posture to tell me that she was putting on a show. Except, I never found it and damn, I tried.

When I'd go after a woman in the past, it was all about in-the-moment lust and attraction. It always wore off after the evening. There was never a pull to *stay*, never a moment to want to learn more about them.

And because of that, I've never been in a relationship. I've never wanted to.

One night, and then I move on.

"So, do you want to talk about it?" Jon, asks during our session.

"Do I want to talk to you about the fact that I seem to have found my match?" I quip.

Jon has been my therapist for the past two years, long enough to understand my trauma but not long enough for me to be healed from it. I'm working on it, I am, but it takes time. And willingness.

"Yes." He looks down at his notepad before continuing. "You spent most of this session talking about this woman you met, and this is the first time you're talking about a relation-ship outside of your friendships."

"It is?"

Jon just nods and waits for me to respond.

"I don't know what else to say..."

"Do you fear that your upbringing will hinder your ability to be emotionally available for her?"

"Fuck, Jon, hit me where it hurts why don't ya." I press a hand to my heart. "I don't know."

He scribbles in his notepad, which used to make me anxious. I was always nervous about saying something that would lead to him dropping me as his client. If I let down my guard with him, I was constantly worried he'd say "good luck with your life," and then I'd be left to pick up the pieces. Again.

He hasn't done that yet, and I've come to trust that he won't, which is a part of this whole therapy work that I've been doing. Not everyone I meet and develop a relationship with will leave me, or choose to only keep me around when something is needed.

Jon asks a few more questions but mostly listens for the remaining time in our session.

On therapy days, I like to go home and not talk to anyone after having spent the last hour talking about myself. But today, I have to go to Emmett's house to celebrate his actual birthday.

When I get there, the door is unlocked, so I let myself in.

And proceed to scare the shit out of Emmett, causing him to spill his coffee.

"You're early," he mutters.

"It's nice to see you too, lover-boy," I tease.

Emmett groans as he wipes up the last bit of spilled coffee. "The nickname is sticking, huh?"

Of course it is. The guy hasn't been interested in anyone in the year that I've known him and now that he has it bad for Cassie, I have to tease him for it.

And also, being the best friend that I am, I remind him to invite Cassie (and Lucy) over tonight before they have to go to work.

When Marcy, Max, and Lane come over, Emmett warns all of us to keep shut about an article that was published today. I don't understand why he's upset about it since he's in the news frequently. He and Cassie were caught leaving out the back door of the venue, the same way Lucy and I left his party, except photographers were ready for him. He should have known, even with being in the back, there was a high probability of him getting his photo taken. It *was* his birthday party, and him being seen with a new woman is huge news. Cassie's face isn't visible in the photo, so it's not like anyone will find out who she is unless someone tips them off.

I want to tell him that he's worrying about nothing, but he leaves the room to take a call from his Mom before I can say anything.

"So, it looked like you had fun last night," Max says to me, low enough that no one else overhears.

"I don't know what you're talking about." I shrug, but I can feel eyes from the others on me.

"There may be low lights in Moonlight Club, but it was still bright enough for me to see who was on your lap."

"Do you have a point?" I ask, irritated. He's never asked me about a girl.

"Just be careful. That's Cassie's best friend. Are you sure you can't fuck with someone else?"

"That's not..." I shake my head. What Max is saying should upset me, but I know he's coming from a good place. "Thanks for the advice, man," I say and stand from my seat, making my way to the island to sit on a stool instead. If I stayed where I was, Max would rile me up, and I don't want to say something I'd regret.

My friends see me as the guy who hooks up with a different woman every weekend, and I've *let* them because it's true. It's been a few months since I last slept with a woman, mostly due to the anxiety of this filming season coming to a close and work ramping up, but they don't think that I have what it takes to be there for someone for longer than an evening.

Not that they've ever come out and said that, but they don't have to.

Lucy

Just parked!

I glance down at my phone and smile, the weight of Max's words still heavy on my shoulders, but lighter now knowing that soon I'll be able to talk to Lucy.

My heart is racing, and my mind won't stop going over a million different ways that this relationship could go. Did last night mean anything to her? Or is she really not interested in me? Will she back out on our date?

I run a hand through my hair and sigh just as the front door opens.

Using all my will power, I remain facing the kitchen. Lucy will see me, and if she wants to talk to me, she can. But if she wants to stay with Cassie, she can do that as well.

A moment later, I feel a presence at my side.

"Hi," Lucy whispers.

I glance at her and whisper back, "Hey, pretty girl."

A light blush creeps up her neck to match the red top she's wearing.

She tells me about her day. Hours could go by, and I'd be a happy man, just listening to her.

Other people meander over, and I resist the urge to grab Lucy in front of them, to claim her as mine. She's *mine*. Lane can't have her, Max can't have her, just me. If she's going to date anyone in our group, it's going to be me.

My low-key approach works out for a while. Everything *was* going great until Lane started to flirt with Lucy right in front of me. She's sitting next to me, and I can't do anything about it. She's laughing, and it pierces my heart to hear someone else make her laugh.

So I do what any normal person would.

I ruin the mood.

"Cassie!" I call, already regretting what I'm about to do, but it's too late now.

She looks at me, nodding for me to continue.

"What'd you think of the article?" I refrain from grimacing, knowing that Emmett is going to be mad at me. But he'll get over it. And on the bright side, Lane walks to the other side of the room, away from Lucy.

"Tyler," Emmett stares my way, giving me his warning glare.

Can't stop now, I suppose.

"I thought it was funny, to be honest. Emmett hasn't had his face in the tabloids for a few months."

Cassie looks around the room at everyone and says, "Oh, um. There's a first time for everything I suppose. I'm just glad it didn't show my face."

She continues to eat her pizza as her gaze drops to the floor, and that's when I *really* start to regret bringing it up and putting her on the spot.

"You're a dick, Tyler," Emmett says.

"I just wanted to talk about the elephant in the room, so you're welcome." I shrug. "You've been so worried about what she thought about it, I thought I'd ask."

It's my way of saying "I'm sorry" for right now without actually saying it. I'll apologize later to Emmett. First, I need to find time to speak to Lucy before she leaves.

Luckily, I get a few moments alone with her as she's getting ready to walk out the door.

"Why did you say that?" Lucy whisper-yells while slipping on her shoes.

"I don't know. I have this thing where I tend to say things without thinking about them, and sometimes it doesn't work out in my favor." I look at the ground, not wanting to see the way she's looking at me. I don't need her disgust, or pity, or whatever feeling she would have toward me.

"Sometimes?"

Lucy nudges my shoulder to get me to look at her, and instead of seeing negativity, I just see her. Her bright green eyes staring at me and a small smile on her face.

"I'm working on it," I say with a shrug.

"I believe you."

And it's those three words that have me smiling for the rest of the night.

5
LUCY

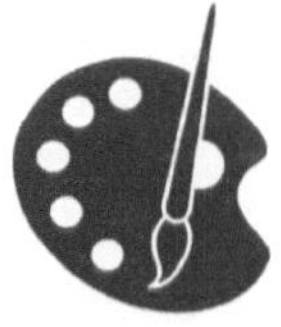

BECAUSE OF OUR NON-STOP texting over the past week, I've learned a lot about Tyler.

His favorite color is red, which influenced his choice of favorite band to be the Red Hot Chili Peppers.

He has watched *Lost* five times.

He eats a savory breakfast.

He broke his ribs during a fight in his junior year of high school.

And he even told me about his parents, or lack thereof, and that he had to learn how to take care of himself at an early age.

In return, I told him about my own lack of parents, but that was due to the multitude of siblings I had. I not only took care of myself, but also my younger siblings. It was something we could semi-relate on, something that brought more depth to our relationship.

We planned our date for Thursday night. I didn't have to work, and Tyler was able to make sure the evening catering was done by his team. That's another thing I found out: he leads catering at January Studios. We've worked across the street from one another and never knew it.

"So, are you going to tell me where we are going?" I ask as we drive down a dirt road to what looks like the middle of nowhere.

"We are almost there, I promise," Tyler says. He reaches over the console to thread his fingers with mine.

He squeezes slightly and my nerves dissipate. Excitement replaces the dread as we turn to the left and slow to a stop.

"Wait here for a moment," Tyler tells me, then hops out of the car. He opens the back seat to take a bag out, then disappears.

A few minutes later, he reappears, opening my door and motioning for me to follow him.

His hand finds mine, and after he interlaces our fingers, he guides me to where he has a blanket laid out in the middle of a field of poppies, lilacs, and lots of other white and yellow and purple flowers. It's a perfect late-summer afternoon, with a slight wind that brings smells of citrus, and woodsy, and honey to my nose.

How did I miss this field? Was I paying attention to the clouds or the wrong side of the road? Was I too worried about how this date would go?

Regardless, there's a field of wildflowers in front of me, and I'm speechless.

"I take that as a good sign that you're impressed," Tyler whispers into my ear.

"How do you know about this place?" I turn to him to find him watching my expression.

"I, uh, might know a guy. And he lets me use his land when I need to come and think or have a moment to myself."

We walk forward until we're on the blanket, and then Tyler sits down, pulling me with him.

"And you're bringing me here? To your spot?" I ask, suddenly aware of how close we are to one another.

"Believe me, I'm surprised too."

"What do you mean?" I ask.

"Do you feel this way with everyone?" Tyler blurts.

I'm silent, speechless yet again, not sure how to answer his question. Of course I don't feel this way with everyone. I haven't *ever* felt this way with someone.

"Sorry, that was...there I go, saying the first thing that comes to my mind." Tyler drops his eyes to his lap.

"What if I told you no?" I admit. "What if I told you that it scares me to think about how you haven't left my mind?"

"Shit, pretty girl, that's... uh..." Tyler blushes, and if that's not the hottest thing, I don't know what is.

"Look, I said the first thing on my mind, so now we are tied," I say.

He leans over, grabs my jaw with a free hand, and tugs my lips to his without a second thought. It ends as quickly as it started, then Tyler lays down on the blanket.

"Lay down," he says, so I do.

Our hands are interlaced between us, and I look over at him, expecting to meet his gaze, but he's looking at the sky.

"Stop looking at me," Tyler says, his lips curled up in a smile.

"How do you know I'm looking at you?" I tease.

His head falls to the left as he says, "Because somehow I've managed to find myself aware of you at all times and can feel you looking at me. Look at the sky."

"Say please," I tease again.

"You're trouble, pretty girl. *Please* look at the sky," he says as he moves our hands closer to my side to pinch me.

"Ah, Tyler, okay, okay." I laugh and turn my head to look at the sky. "What—"

"Look at the clouds. Tell me what you see," he interrupts.

"What are we? Teenagers?"

"Will you please just trust me?" Tyler looks at me again, his eyes soft as he requests for me to indulge him.

So, I turn to look to the sky. And for a few moments, I don't see anything but fluffy white clouds. And I'm about to give up, not being able to make out any patterns in the abstractness, when I see a small outline of a shape that opens up my mind to the rest of the sky.

"I see water, waves of water," I start, watching the clouds move at a snail's pace above me. "And birds, flying overhead as a boat travels the water. There's something large, maybe an island, or a city, but something in the distance that the boat is traveling to."

Tyler is quiet as I continue on about the clouds, my mind picturing different scenes as the sky changes in front of us. And even once it begins to darken and the clouds turn gray and move quicker with the wind, I remain still and tell him the pictures I see.

Rain begins to drop and flutter around us. The light mist turns into a downpour making it impossible to keep my eyes open without blinking away the precipitation.

I hardly notice Tyler stand until he's hauling me up and throwing the blanket over his shoulder.

We run to the car, and it's not until we are breathing heavily in the front seat that I see the time.

"How did an hour pass?" I say, appalled that I just spent that long doing nothing but staring at the sky.

Tyler just shrugs, pushing a hand through the wet strands of his hair until they are out of his face.

"Why? Why did you bring me here to watch clouds?" I ask, my mind racing as I try to come up with the reason myself and fail.

"You told me you needed inspiration, and I thought that if this is where I think best, it might help you too."

I open my mouth to say something, but all words about how I feel are gone. My internal alarm should be blaring with the way I'm feeling right now. Tyler not only showed me his special place, but he shared this part of his life to help me. To help my art. All because I told him when we met how I didn't have a clue what to paint.

I *know* I shouldn't be feeling like this. Why is my heart wanting to let him have a piece of it so soon? It's too soon, right? I *never* felt like this with Jake, or any other ex. Sure, I had strong feelings, but I never fell for them like I am for Tyler. The party where we met was only last weekend, and this is only the third time I've seen him, but every time I stare at him or he talks to me my stomach flutters.

"I like you, Tyler," is what I say after a beat of silence, the tension brimming in the air.

He smiles, says, "I know," then starts the car and drives us back toward the city.

6
TYLER

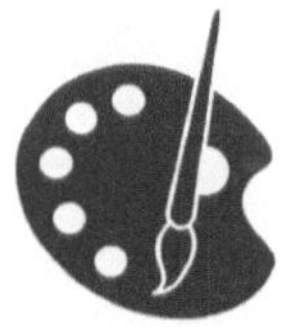

"Tyler," Lucy practically screams into the phone on Friday afternoon.

She told me when I dropped her off yesterday that she was planning to spend her day at the studio painting.

"I think I did it."

"You did it?"

"I did it," she says again, her excitement rubbing off on me.

"I'm so proud of you, pretty girl. Text me the address?" I ask, already walking out the door of my office and toward my car.

"Of what? The studio? Why?"

"I want to come see you. I want to tell you congratulations in person, if that's alright."

"Oh," Lucy says. "Yeah, of course. I'd, um, love that actually."

"See you soon."

If I've learned anything about Lucy over the past week, it's that she's persistent and will keep trying until everything is perfect.

I also learned that her favorite color is green and she prefers bagels to toast. She would rather drink black coffee than tea, but if she had to drink tea, then she would choose green tea. That detail threw me for a loop.

She prefers the sunset over the sunrise most days, unless there's coffee and pastries involved. Tuesday night, on a call when we were talking about anything and everything, Lucy opened up more about her art. That night I didn't go to bed until four in the morning and ended up drinking eight cups of coffee the next day. I told myself I'd be more responsible, go to bed at a reasonable time, but after our date last night, we stayed up texting again. Not as late this time, since she was planning to spend all day in the studio and I wanted to make sure she was rested, but late enough to make this drive feel like it's taking ages to get to my destination.

It's nearly four in the afternoon when I get to the studio, and I realize I know this area of town because it's close to a lot of restaurants I used to frequent on dates. I've already made a mental note to talk to Jon about my dating history and how to make sure it doesn't affect what I have going on with Lucy because I don't know how to tell her that I had a habit of seeing new women regularly.

I still need to talk to Jon about the lack of emotional availability that he asked me about. I have plenty of emotions around Lucy, but I'm not always open to sharing them.

That's a problem for my therapist and a conversation that will take at least a few sessions.

"Hi, you," Lucy greets as I walk toward the door that she is holding open for me.

"Hi, pretty girl," I lean in and kiss her gently.

"Now, you can't judge them. Okay? It's still an early concept, but it's the first time I've had all three pieces match," Lucy says as she guides me to the room she's been working out of.

"I am not an art connoisseur, Luce, so don't worry. I'm here to support you, okay?"

She nods quickly, as if she's convincing herself that that's why I'm here. There's no ulterior motive but that.

We weave through the building, passing various rooms where other people are working on pieces. Some of the rooms house a different medium; such as woodworking or ceramics, but most of the studio seems to be for painters.

"What kind of building is this?" I ask Lucy as we round a corner.

"What do you mean?" She slows her pace enough to lace her fingers in mine.

"I just noticed a lot of people here, I kind of thought you'd work in a private studio or something."

"Oh, I wish," Lucy chuckles. "Maybe if I get a permanent spot at the gallery, then I can use their rented studio space. This was the only place I could afford, that's why it's out of the city."

"And is there anyone in the studio with you today? Or is it just you?"

"Just me. Since Kelly and my ex, Jake, left, no one has taken their spot."

"They both left? At the same time?" I ask.

Lucy nods and says, "Jake cheated on me with Kelly."

"He what?" I stop in my tracks, pulling us both to a standstill. "Why are you not furious about this? Was this a while ago?"

Lucy shakes her head. "It was maybe a month ago? I don't know. I am mad? But also relieved?" She tugs on my hand to pull us toward her studio. "We dated for six months, but the entire time we were together it never felt like *this*."

"And by *this* you mean?" I ask, because I need to know.

She drops her eyes to the floor, but I can see her biting her lip before she looks back at me. "Okay, so you know how I called you earlier? To tell you about my paintings?"

I nod.

"I would have never wanted to do that with Jake."

"You wouldn't have wanted to call him about your art? Was he not an artist too? Wouldn't he have wanted to be there for you?"

"That's the thing, he wouldn't have. He painted realistic landscapes, which are basically the opposite of my abstract ones. He didn't understand my art, and he never tried to. So even though we spent a lot of time together in the studio, we didn't talk about art outside of it." She shrugs.

"But Lucy, you love art."

"And that's why it's different." She smiles. "I should have known he'd go for Kelly."

"Why?"

"She painted portraits." She chuckles.

"Fuckers," I say, laughing with her.

"Yeah, right. Fuckers." She smiles wide and my heart flips in my chest. "Okay, this is me here." Lucy opens the door to her left.

Her paintings are the first thing I see when we enter the room. I don't know what I was expecting, but three giant canvases weren't it. I thought maybe three 8inx12in canvas paintings, or maybe a little larger. These are easily four feet wide and seven feet tall.

"Wow," I say, walking closer to look at the details of each painting. There are assorted blobs of color, most of them varying shades of blue and purple. It's a slight gradient from the leftmost painting to the right, with something I can't quite make out tying it all together.

"So," Lucy stands next to me and whispers.

My gaze drops to her. Her hands are clasped, and she's biting her bottom lip (something I've noticed she does a lot) while her attention stays on her paintings.

"They don't match, do they?" Lucy asks, sighing because I'm taking too long to comment on how speechless I am about her work.

"I see it," I say, looking back at the paintings and tilting my head to look from a different angle.

"Really?" Lucy asks, hope lining her tone.

"Maybe." I wince, and she playfully shoves me. I lose my balance and almost fall into a puddle of spilled paint. "I'm kidding, no need to be violent, pretty girl."

The way her cheeks turn the prettiest pink at me calling her that is definitely in my top five favorite things. The other four are cooking, spending time with friends, watching random movies, and being around Lucy. Oh, look, two spots for her.

"It's inspired by the date you took me on," she half mumbles as she walks from the first painting to the second, pointing out various shapes. As soon as she does that, I can see and understand how they're all connected.

"Are you saying I'm your inspiration?" I bump into her shoulder.

"You *could* say I am a little bit inspired, yes," Lucy says, turning to face me.

"And what would you say if I told you I'm a little bit inspired and would very much like to kiss the hell out of you?" I begin to walk toward her, and she does what I expect: walks back until she hits a wall.

My hands move to either side of her head to box her in.

"Has anyone ever told you that you're a little forward?" Lucy squeals out as I plant slow kisses along her neck.

"Mm, you might have before," I respond as I switch to the other side of her neck. "Is that a problem?"

"I—ah—" She moans as I move my hand and grab her ass, pushing her into me. "You're going to get me in trouble."

"I locked the door," I say, my mouth traveling down her body.

"Tyler," Lucy says.

"L. u. c. y," I draw out her name with each kiss I plant on her body, but I decide at the last minute to travel back up and press my lips against hers.

She sighs into me, wrapping her arms around my neck before moving one hand to play with my hair.

When I break our kiss a moment later, I rest my forehead on hers and keep my eyes closed as I listen to our labored breathing. The smell of lemon and paint and lavender fill my noise all at once, and I want to bottle it up and spray it over my pillows. Better yet...

"I need you in my home, in my bed. Your smell is killing me, pretty girl. Come over tonight. Stay the night. Let me cook you dinner," I say, practically begging.

"Cook me dinner, huh? So you *can* cook?" Lucy jokes. I pinch her side before capturing her mouth one more time.

"Just say yes, *please*."

"Okay." She smiles, and now I have to figure out what I'm going to cook for dinner and how I'm going to get my mind to understand that whatever is going on with Lucy doesn't have to be a temporary thing.

7
TYLER

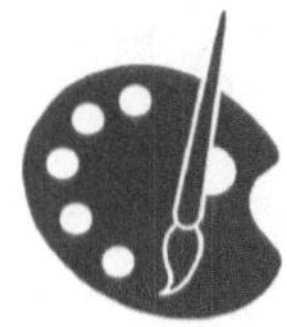

"So, this is where you live," Lucy muses as she walks around my apartment.

"It's impressive, I know." I lean against the counter and cross my arms, enjoying the sight of her in my space.

"It *is* impressive, if you must know. It's way bigger than my apartment with Cassie," she says as she thumbs through a stack of books in my living room.

"Just wait until you see the bedroom."

Lucy peeks over her shoulder to give me a *look*, then continues to snoop through my things. I watch and take deep breaths to calm the nerves building inside.

My foot has been bouncing to try and shake the negative thoughts from my head, but it's not working. So I slipped away earlier to send a text to Jon with an *"SOS."* Jon texted back with his typical therapist-advice; be honest, speak from the heart, and breathe. I don't normally text him with problems, but then again, it's never been this urgent. Even though most of me is happy that Lucy is here tonight, there is still a small sliver that wants to push her away, to tell her I'm sick or something to get her to leave.

Just because Lucy is here doesn't mean I have to mold myself into someone I'm not. On the flip side, I *like* who I am when I'm around her. I'm not Loud Tyler, Annoying Tyler, Tyler That Won't Shut Up. To her, I'm me. And whatever version that is, she seems to like.

"You okay, Tyler?" Lucy brushes against my side.

"Yeah, pretty girl, I'm okay." I smile, knowing that my emotions are blatant on my face.

"We could talk about it, you know, if you want..." She trails off, giving me the space to tell her if I want.

"This isn't the kind of conversation you have on an empty stomach."

"Put me to work, chef," Lucy says as she stands up a little straighter. She lightens the weight in my chest without even knowing it, just from joking around and being herself.

"I can be a little bossy. You sure you want to help?" I ask, walking to the fridge. I've decided that we'll make a hash since it's simple and can consist of a conglomerate of things.

"I can handle it." Lucy is doing a little dance, her smile is big, her eyes crinkle, and I find myself smiling and laughing at how adorable she is. I set the ingredients down on the counter in front of of her and jokingly slap her ass.

"I'm sure you can," I say.

"Just tell me what to do, chef."

"You know, I used to want to be a chef," I tell her. "Also, you can start with cutting these."

Lucy grabs a knife and starts to cube the potatoes. "When you were a child? Or is this recent?"

"For as long as I can remember, honestly." I take a few carrots to peel and cube. "I had to learn at an early age how to cook for myself and my mom. I remember turning ten and being tired of frozen meals and cereal, so I started watching videos on how to cook. First it was basic things like pasta dishes or an omelet. The obsession grew from there, it became my escape."

Lucy listens as I tell her my story. And being in my element, cooking, helps get past the emotional block.

"What next? I'm done with the potatoes," Lucy says. She pushes them into a bowl.

"You can cut these peppers. Make them thin strips."

"Yes, chef," she says. "Where was your dad?"

"Who knows." I shrug. "He wasn't around much when I was young but would pop in every once in a while. I think he was looking for money and when he wasn't getting any, he stopped showing up. But honestly, I don't remember him, so it doesn't matter much."

"It matters, Ty." Lucy touches my arm and I nod, not having the words to reply.

Lucy goes back to chopping, and I chop the bacon. "My mom…" I start, but I find it hard to talk about her. I always do, even with Jon. It's taken my therapist almost our whole time for me to talk about her.

Instead of saying something, interjecting another question, or telling me that I don't have to talk about it, Lucy stays silent. The rhythm of her knife matched with mine calms me me enough that when I gather up all the ingredients to take over to the stove, I tell her about my mom.

"My mom wasn't really around much. That's the main reason why I started cooking for myself. Hell, I did most things for myself. I forged her signature so I could go on field trips, I started working as soon as I could to help give her money, I did everything I could to try and help her be home more. It was just the two of us, and I wanted her there. With me."

"And she wasn't?" Lucy asks, though she probably already knows where this is going.

I shake my head. "I mean, some nights, yes. She would come home early, we would play a board game..." I chuckle, reminiscing. "It was fun. I felt like she wanted to be there with me. But as I started to get older, she stopped coming back home. I had friends, luckily, which helped, but it wasn't the same." I pause, taking a deep breath to calm the rising anxiety in my chest. "Everyone I've loved has left me, so I don't really try anymore."

Lucy wraps her arms around my waist and lays her head on my back. "You do have people that love you, you know?"

I turn the heat down on the stove before turning around to face her. "I do, but it's still ingrained in me. It's why I am the way I am when I'm around my friends. I think I'm so worried about people leaving that I make sure that I'm the type of person they wouldn't want to leave."

Lucy reaches up to cup my face, and I lean into her touch.

"And you're the only one I've told that to," I admit.

"The only one?" Lucy's eyes widen.

"Well, and Jon, my therapist. He, uh, helps me talk through things. Like you and stuff." I turn back to the stove to stir the hash now that the bacon is crispy and the vegetables are soft, then divide it between two bowls.

"Interesting topics..." Lucy hums.

"You are an important topic for me to discuss, pretty girl." I lean over and press a kiss to her forehead. "Let's eat, and we can keep talking."

"That sounds good to me." Lucy smiles. "How did you get into catering?"

"I couldn't afford to go to school to be a chef, but I did work for a catering company for a few years instead of going to college. It was still around food, and turns out I'm not half bad at it. So, when January Studios needed someone to run their catering department, I applied."

"And you got it." Lucy grins.

"And I got it." I nod. "It was kind of like fate, to be honest. I was at a low point in my life, working for another company, my mom kept asking for money, and I couldn't find my way out of it... you know?"

"I believe in fate," Lucy says, and I find myself wondering if she thinks that us meeting is fate. If out of the billions of people in the world, we were meant to find each other.

For the rest of dinner, we talk about our pasts. I did enough talking while we were cooking, so Lucy holds the conversation for most of the hour. She tells me about how she grew up, when she fell in love with painting, and what it's been like to live in the city.

By the time we're finished eating, I could ace a pop quiz if it only contained facts about Lucy.

I still don't know if this will work, if I'll be able to be there for someone else without the worry of them leaving. It's only been one week since I met Lucy, and if I didn't feel something different between us, I wouldn't have texted her after the first night. She wouldn't have my number.

But there's still a part of me that's putting on a mask, showing her what I *think* the real me is.

Lucy nudges my foot under the table to get my attention. "Are you going to show me your bedroom?"

I huff and smile, then proceed to throw her over my shoulder and take her to my room.

8
LUCY

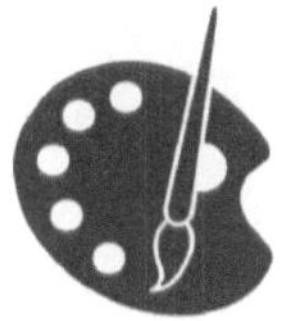

"Put me down, Tyler!" I demand as he carries me to his bedroom.

At least my view is nice, hanging over his back.

"As you wish, pretty girl."

The next moment, I'm tossed onto a cloud, a.k.a. his bed. It's so soft my body wants to sink into it and sleep for days.

"Tired?" Tyler asks, ever so perceptive.

"I'm not *too* tired," I respond.

"Good because I have plans for us tonight."

Tyler sheds his shirt in one smooth movement, and my eyes drop to his chest and the V leading into his jeans.

"Eyes on me, Luce," he says as he crawls on top of me. I follow his direction and lay down under him as his hands come to either side of my head.

My hands find his bare back and I pull him closer until his mouth finds mine.

An electric current runs from the point of contact down my spine, sending signals of pleasure through my nerves. Every thought is consumed by him at this moment. Every breath stolen.

"Does this scare you?" I ask in between kisses, my breathing fast and shallow.

His lips move to my chin, peppering small kisses to try and distract me.

"Does what scare me?" Tyler asks, switching to the other side of my face. A hand cups my breast over my shirt and I'm mad at myself for having a conversation when I'd much rather be taking my clothes off.

"Us."

Tyler pauses and looks at me. "Are you asking if it's not normal to hide our relationship from our best friends and pretend I don't feel the way I feel about you?"

"No. I mean, yes, that's not normal." I chuckle, bringing a hand to cover my face. "What I mean is are you scared that this isn't very casual when we've only known each other for a week?"

His hand moves to grab mine, and as he brings it back down, he presses a soft kiss to my knuckles.

"Oh. Yes, I'm terrified. This feels like a rubber band. It's holding us together, no matter how many layers we add on. What if I do something or say something and fucks it up?"

"You will," I say, reaching for his head. I pull him toward me, bringing his forehead to mine. "But if you're there for the important moments, that's all that matters."

"I'll need to write that down. I can be forgetful sometimes."

"I'll be here to remind you if you need it."

Tyler finds my lips again. With each kiss, each swipe of his tongue, each grasp of his hand, something changes between us. The lust, the passion, the intentionality of our relationship, it's all there.

And as the night progresses, and we stay up too late, I can't help but wonder if I'm falling for him too fast. If I'm setting myself up for a broken heart by leaping into this headfirst. There's something holding him back, and I can't figure out what it is.

9
TYLER

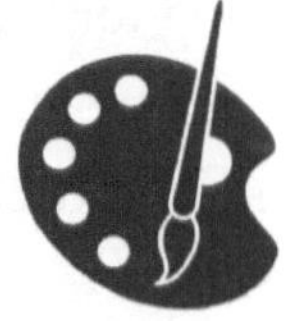

It's been three months since Lucy and I started seeing each other. All of my time is split between work and Lucy, and we might be neglecting our friends. It's not that we are trying to keep our relationship a secret, it's more that we are figuring out what we are together in private first.

With Emmett and Cassie doing their thing and most of us being fairly certain they're together, Lucy and I have decided to keep things to ourselves.

I mean, we haven't discussed it. But I'm also not seeing anyone else, so to me it's obvious.

"Can we try to leave in a few minutes?" Lucy's voice comes from down the hall.

"Yes, I'll be ready soon," I holler back.

She's been staying the night frequently instead of being alone at her apartment. Jon shared his hesitations with me when I saw him last because when I'm around others, I tend to shut down and build a barrier around myself. Or I put on a mask and act like the Tyler everyone seems to like. I don't want to do that with Lucy, which is why I enlisted Jon's help. He provided me with a few coping mechanisms. The past few nights, I've been trying them.

The first thing I did was tell Lucy ways I cope best, so that she could help. Or at least try to help. Sometimes I want to be alone, or I may seem like I want to be left alone, but deep down, I want the opposite.

Lucy shouldn't take the burden for me, but I don't want her to be left in the dark if my mood suddenly shifts. If I end up in a spiral and get in my own thoughts, she needs to know that it's not about her.

Then, I practiced. Whenever I started to feel overwhelmed or triggered, I tried the methods Jon taught me. They helped, a little bit, depending on where I was. My work environment isn't the best, as everyone expects me to be loud and in their face.

What I'm coming to find from therapy is to not look at that persona as a different part of me but to look at it as a side that only certain people get to see. It's my way to close off emotions, to show a hardened outside.

Just when I'm about to leave the bedroom to go meet Lucy in the kitchen, my phone rings. There's only a few people in my life that still call me.

And by the name on the screen, I can tell it's not going to be a great conversation. It would be *so* simple to press decline, to ignore the person on the other end of the line. I wouldn't have to deal with this impending feeling of dread, or the tightness in my chest, or think about how it's difficult for me to talk a full breath. If I could avoid this trigger, I would, but I know she'd just call me back later, so I sit down on the bed before accepting.

"Hi, Mom. It's been a while," I say, my gaze steady on the floor in front of me.

"Oh, has it? Did we not just talk last week?"

I hold back in a sigh even though I want nothing more than to release the disappointment. "It's been a little over six months."

"Oh, Tyty, it's more recent than that, I'm sure."

Ugh, the nickname I loathe mixed with the fact that she thinks our last conversation was more recent tells me what she's calling about without me having to ask.

"How are you? Are you still in Wyoming?" I ask, trying to skirt the subject.

"No, I'm in Montana now. But I'm coming home soon, and I'd like to see you."

There's ruckus on the other end, and I know I should be sad for her, should ask questions about where she is, but I've worked *so* hard to create boundaries and to not feel responsible for her.

"Sure, Mom."

"Great, Tyty. Someone else needs to borrow my phone, so I'll give you a ring when I find myself in the area. Once I get enough money, I'll be there to see you."

Well, sounds like she spent all the money I gave her last time when I told her it would, in fact, be the last time.

"Sounds good, Mom. Bye," I say and hang up the phone without waiting for a response.

I drop my head into my hands and close my eyes, letting out the big sigh I'd been holding in. The only times I've heard from my Mom over the past decade have been when she needed money. She calls about once a year, sometimes more, but this time last year, I told her I'm done. When we talked last, she didn't ask for money and I felt hopeful, but my gut was queasy as soon as she greeted this time. I *knew* money was what she was after, or will be after when we talk next. I need to focus on myself and my growth, not worried if my mom will call me for a reason other than her own gain.

The bed sinks and a hand rubs my back, followed by a kiss to the side of my head.

I lean into Lucy's touch. Moments pass, and my breathing returns to a normal pace. I find myself conflicted with my mom.

I want her to be okay, but I also want to be okay. I want to have this life, with Lucy, to not have to worry about my past and my baggage and the constant worry if I'll always end up alone.

"Okay, I'm ready." I lift my head after one last deep breath and stand, reaching my hand down to help Lucy up.

She takes it, and I pull her into a hug. "You sure? We don't have to go this week. I can always get groceries delivered."

"I'm sure. Fresh air always helps." Which is true.

And that's how we find ourselves at the farmer's market ten minutes later. We peruse the stalls, each of us carrying a tote bag to haul items in.

Farmer's markets are always busy, so I should have known I'd see people from my past. Women from my past, to be exact. Not just one, or two, either. We've walked down two aisles of tents and I've already seen six different women I know intimately.

I take Lucy's hand and guide us in the other direction, not wanting to run into them. Lucy and I haven't had the *talk* yet about our pasts and this is not the way I want it to come out.

There wasn't anyone before Lucy. I've never had a girlfriend; if we were to put labels on our relationship, she'd be the first. My lack of experience means I'm not quite sure when to bring the subject up, or if she even wants a label.

Unfortunately, it looks like the universe hates me today because as we are gathering lettuce and vegetables for the week, a blonde woman dressed in a short floral summer dress grabs my arm and yanks me toward her.

"Tyler! Oh my gosh, it's been ages since I've seen you. And by ages I mean a few months," she says. Her hand rubs my arm up and down.

I'm frozen in place. It takes Lucy wrapping her arm around me and giving me a slight tug to shake me out of my shock.

"Hi, I'm Lucy." Lucy holds me tight, her nails digging into my arm.

Is she doing it on purpose? Probably.

"Oh, excuse my manners. I'm Lilly. I'm an ex of Tyler's." The woman I now remember as Lilly shakes Lucy's hand. "Well, not technically an ex. I could never tame this man. He never called me back," she says, looking at me with her lips in a pout.

"Oh, really? Well, what a shame," Lucy says with a smile, her daggers still leaving little half moons in my skin.

I look at Lucy, then at Lilly, and back, wondering if I should say something. I should say something, right? It's not like I even remember Lilly or the night we shared. Maybe that's the problem. I was immune to any feelings associated with the women I was sleeping with, just using them to cope with whatever fucked up feelings I was dealing with. Our time together never lasted more than a few hours, and she's right, I never call. We don't exchange contact information; that's how I keep it casual.

"Well, we should, uh, keep shopping," I say, feeling a giant pit in my stomach grow with each passing moment.

It's terribly hot outside. Pair that with the anxiety left over from talking to my mom and a little bit of regret both from choosing this damn farmer's market this morning and sleeping with women that like to shop at farmer's markets, and you get a very uncomfortable morning.

I dip my head in a goodbye and drag Lucy away from the stand. We don't stop until we reach the car. Our hands are still interlaced, but the only sound coming from us is the swishing of our bags of food.

I'm already starting to fuck it up, and I know Lucy is being patient, but I find myself getting more and more anxious about what will be the one thing that will finally be the last layer to break the rubber band.

10
LUCY

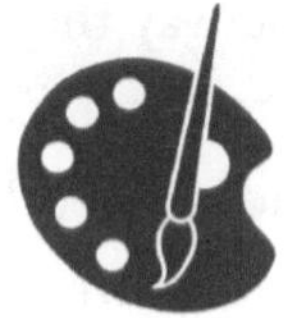

Aren't farmer's markets supposed to be fun? There's nice weather, good food, nice people. That's basically the definition of fun.

You want to know the one thing that's not in that definition? Seeing a million of your boyfriend's ex-partners within the span of an hour. Okay, I can't confirm every woman that made eyes at Tyler was an ex-partner and he's not *technically* my boyfriend, but that doesn't change the fact that I simply seemed like another woman on his arm.

"Lucy, talk to me, please," Tyler says once we get into the car.

"It's fine, Tyler, really," I say, trying to hold it together.

Because it is fine. I shouldn't be upset about this. He didn't do anything wrong. We are just friends. But we are also a lot more, and I'm finding myself in this constant state of wondering if he feels the same way about us.

"Lucy," Tyler draws out my name and places a hand on my thigh.

"Tyler." I look at him and try to hold back a smile, but it breaks free as soon as I see a smile form on his face.

"I've worn you down once, I can do it again. Tell me what's wrong, pretty girl."

He knows my weaknesses, that's for sure.

"I see those women, the way they look at you, and I can't help but compare myself to them. To how much of you they might have had, and I know you call me, and text me, and I practically never leave your apartment these days, but I can't help but feel insecure about whatever *this* is between us."

He nods and takes his hand back from my thigh. He rakes his hair away from his face, but it's no use because the stray pieces fall right back where they were.

"I'm not the Tyler they know, the Tyler they were with. You know that, right?"

I nod. He's not, from what I can gather at least, but I don't know him outside of how he acts around me.

"You'll have to help me out, Luce, this is my first relationship. I don't know how this works. There's never been someone in my life that I could call my girlfriend or my partner. There's no one, besides you, that I've wanted to make mine. Officially mine. I don't want to move too fast if you don't want that, and I don't know if I'm supposed to call you my girlfriend. I don't know if you want to be my girlfriend."

"Well, for one," I say as I place my hand over his to stop him from rambling and make sure he's looking at me before

I continue, "I have been at your place more than mine for the past few months, which I would consider to be moving fairly fast. And two, you wouldn't know because you haven't asked me yet."

His lips turn up on either side to form a smile, then his bottom lip disappears as he ponders what I just said. I wait, patiently, until he opens his mouth to ask me the question I already know the answer to.

"Will you be my girlfriend, pretty girl?" Tyler leans over the center console.

I'm able to nod once before his lips are on mine, claiming me for anyone who walks by to see.

"This is one of those important moments, isn't it?" Tyler asks.

I nod again. "I think so."

"Well, we should get home and take advantage of it, don't you think?"

Thirty minutes later due to some traffic, we are finally home.

"Lunch now or later?" I ask, peering into the fridge when we're done putting the groceries away.

"Later," Tyler says. He closes the door and spins me around, pinning me to the fridge. "There's something else I'd rather do now."

His lips capture mine barely a second later. He's hungry for something, but it's not food. Not after the morning we had, and the commitment to each other we've made.

"Bedroom," I whisper and he nods but continues to kiss me as we make our way out of the kitchen.

We fumble down the hallway, kissing and laughing until we end up in the bedroom. I'm very grateful we didn't run into a laundry basket or something because that would have killed the mood for sure.

"I've been thinking of you naked in bed all morning," Tyler says as he pulls down my pants.

"I was *just* naked in bed this morning." I reach down to help take off my shirt, and he takes off his.

Within a minute, we are both naked and reaching for one another.

"Mm, wasn't long enough though."

"If it was any longer, we would have never left, Tyler." I reach down to grab his chin to bring his face to meet mine. "Enough talking."

"Whatever you wish, pretty girl."

We kiss, and kiss, and kiss some more. Taking our time to be with each other, with nothing but the sounds of our breaths filling the room. Any negative thought I had earlier dissipates as his hand trails lower, and lower, until his thumb finds my clit.

My back arches, and my nails dig into his back as he inserts one, then two fingers. If Tyler knows one thing, it's how to pleasure a woman, and I find myself reaching climax in record time. My legs shake and my breath quickens as I reach my peak. Tyler captures my moan in his mouth as his fingers begin to slow and are replaced with his cock once he slips on a condom.

"That's it," he whispers into my hair.

"Faster," I plead. "I need more."

He does as I ask, thrusting harder, faster until we both are at the edge, me for the second time.

"Fuck." Tyler drops his head into the crook of my neck as he pushes in and out of me at a slow pace.

"Fuck is right," I say, and we both chuckle.

He pulls out, then lays to the side of me, his hand cusping my cheek.

"You and me, we're something good. And I need you to know I'm working on myself, and I also need you to know that I like you a lot," Tyler says as his thumb caresses my cheek.

"There's nothing wrong with you, Tyler. You don't need to change for me, you know that right? I like you the way you are," I whisper, pressing a hand over his.

"That's the thing. Around you, I'm different. When I'm with others, it's like this other side of me takes over and I say and do things without thinking. I need you to understand that I have *never* felt like this before. I wasn't lying when I said I don't date. I've never felt pulled to date someone, to talk with them for longer than one night before you came along."

"Why? You deserve to be loved, Tyler."

Love. I love him.

And I think he knows that because his thumb stops for a split second but then continues as if nothing happened.

Tyler sighs, then says, "You're magnetic. You walk into a room and everyone smiles just from you being there. The way you continue to show up, and be supportive, while you're dealing with so much on your own plate is something I strive for. You just have this way of bringing out the best in me, and I find myself never wanting to let you go."

"So, then don't let me go, Tyler." I lean in and give him a kiss. "Hold on to me, and don't let me go."

11
TYLER

I look over my shoulder at Emmett who's standing behind me in line for lunch.

"I'm not acting weird," I say and turn back around to grab a sandwich from the fridge.

"Who is it?" Emmett pushes, coming to stand in front of me.

It wouldn't be like me to tell him about Lucy. I'd rather keep my mouth shut and not dive into it right now. Emmett is one of my best friends and doesn't even know that I've been struggling so much. None of my friends do. I've hardly told them about my mom, and that isn't because they don't ask.

Max and Lane stumbled into my life by pure accident. They happened to be at a networking event I was catering with a previous company, and we bonded over our hate for posh food. They were there trying to make connections to promote their casting company to larger studios. I offered to make them something after I served the meal being offered to everyone else, they accepted, we ate together, and exchanged numbers. We met up a few times, when I was able to get away from work. Our time together was mostly spent at bars for the first few years, and then once I started working at the studio, I passed their names along without thinking anything of it.

A month later, they were hired to be the in-house casting team, and our friendships evolved from there. But I still don't have a handle on myself, on my emotions, and I have yet to learn to be open with those I care about. Emmett joined our friend group a little over a year ago. At that point it was too late to say anything.

I don't know how to open up and say, *"Sorry, I had a fucked up past and am just telling you about it now."*

So, I don't. And I avoid any conversation like the one Emmett is trying to have because it would normally require more from me than I'm willing to give.

"You're not going to drop this, are you?" I push past Emmett and start walking to the table where Max and Lane are already sitting.

"Nope, not going to drop it." Emmett sits next to me, slamming his plate down to make a point.

"Not going to drop what?" Max chimes in, but his mouth is full of pasta, so his words come out all garbled.

"Is some girl stalking you again, Tyler?" Lane asks.

I take a bite of my lunch and shake my head. "That was one time."

She really wouldn't take no for an answer when I wouldn't give her my number and showed up at the studio looking for me.

"Tyler is seeing someone and he won't say who." Emmett fills everyone in, and I groan. This is not supposed to be public knowledge.

"You're seeing someone?" Max asks, clearly stunned at the fact that I could have a stable girlfriend.

"Yes, I'm seeing someone, okay? Can we drop it?" I give in and try to eat faster so I can leave.

"Dude, you can't keep stuff like this from your best friends. Who is it?" Lane asks.

My knee bounces, and I find myself unable to meet their gazes when I say, "It's someone you all know."

"Who?" Lane whispers to Max, but it's loud enough that I can hear him, hear them all thinking the same thing.

"How long?" Emmett asks, trying to figure out the puzzle.

"Uh, three months? Somewhere around there?" I answer.

"What was three months ago?" Max asks, his mouth once again full of food.

Lane hums in an attempt to remember. "I'm not sure—"

"My birthday party." Emmett interrupts Lane. "My party was three months ago."

"Oh fuck, dude. Is it who you were with all night?" Max asks, clearly remembering the fact that he saw Lucy straddled on my lap.

I nod in response.

"Who—?" Emmett starts but stops and slaps me in the shoulder instead.

"Hey," I shout. "That's not nice."

"Really, Tyler? Lucy? Is this why you haven't been able to hang out?" Emmett asks.

"Well, this has been fun, boys," I say as I start to stand.

"Nope." Emmett presses my shoulder down, and I slump back into the chair. "Explain."

"You all clearly know now, so there's not much else to explain," I sneer, a hint of anger creeping into my voice.

"Tyler, we've known you for how long? And this is the first relationship you're in? Come on," Lane says.

"It happened fast, okay? She..." I sigh and press my forehead to the table. "She's too good for me, and somehow she likes *me.*"

I admit it without thinking about it, and the entire table is silent for a few beats. The guys have always seen me in a different light, or at least I assume that. To them, I never had a bad day, and I never had issues with women. That was me. I'm a lot of other things too, like a supportive friend, but I've never talked to them about my feelings.

That's what Jon is for.

So, it feels weird to open up to them now. And now that it's out there, I find more words tumbling out before I'm able to stop them.

"You all see me as something else, and I try to be that version of myself. But I'm also trying to be better, and to be more emotionally available," I start, my attention still on the empty plate in front of me. "At least, that's what my therapist tells me to do," I grumble.

"Tyler, you can talk to us, you know. We are here if you need us," Emmett says.

And I know that; I know I could call them up and tell them things. It's not that I don't want to, but I've never had someone to lean on, to be there for me, and I'm having a hard enough time trying to let Lucy be that person that it's difficult to even think about adding more people to the mix.

"Yeah, I know." I look at Emmett. "I know."

He nods but lets me continue talking.

"And with everything that's happened with my mom. She's not great. Well, it's not that, but—" I shake my head, my words not making sense. My hand fidgets with a loose thread in my shirt while my knee bounces. "I don't want to get into that, but yes Lucy and I are dating. But it's private, okay? I don't want anyone to know."

"Want anyone to know what?" Marcy chooses the worst possible time to show up.

Oh, and she's with Cassie. Wonderful.

"That Tyler actually likes pineapple on pizza." Emmett covers for me, looking at me with a knowing smile.

"Ew, Tyler," Cassie says as she sits next to Emmett.

"I like what I like." I shrug.

Now that my heart is out on the table for the guys, I feel...lighter? There's this whole other side of me that they haven't seen, and it became so normal to lock that part of me up. To pretend that I'm less than what I am. That the baggage of my past doesn't influence my behaviors and antics.

Every deep breath I take acts as a reminder that I'm okay, or that I will be okay, and that I'm allowed to take control of my future. Even if there's a chance that it won't be with Lucy.

12
LUCY

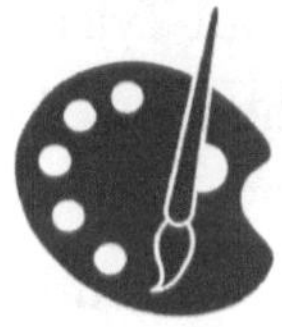

HE SAID HE'D BE here.

"Lucy, you okay?" the director at the art gallery I'm showing at asks me.

"Oh, yes." I pocket my phone, checking the room once again for any sight of Tyler. "Just checking to see if someone I was expecting was going to be here in time."

The director nods and lets me know that the gallery will close in thirty minutes. I hide my concern with a smile as she walks away, then resume fidgeting with a random piece of paper in my hand, folding and unfolding it, as I scan the room.

Tonight was a trial of the actual showcase taking place in a little under two months. We were to bring three pieces that showed our art style while prospective buyers walked through and looked at them. It's supposed to be a preview on what to expect come the real night, when I hope to land a permanent spot in the gallery.

Tyler called me yesterday to tell me that the guys know about us. He didn't seem upset, did he? Did I read him wrong? I would have typically been over at his place, but he had to work late, and I had to work at the diner, so it made more sense to just stay home. I was planning on seeing him today anyway.

Cassie walks back toward me, smiling as she always does when she sees my art. She's the most supportive best friend, and keeping this secret about Tyler is killing me. I want to tell her, and I might have if he showed up tonight, but now I'm not sure.

I mean, we had a *great* weekend. A mind-blowing, unforgettable weekend.

Or maybe I'm the only one that thought that.

Why would he open up to me, tell me his feelings, only to not show up tonight?

Maybe something happened.

Or maybe he's decided that he doesn't want to be in a relationship.

I've texted him a few times, but he hasn't responded. My vision blurs at the edges, and I'm trying my best to not let the tears fall while showing my art. Not yet.

"Sorry I can't celebrate with you more tonight." Cassie side-hugs me. "This art is really beautiful, Luce."

"It's okay, I already knew you had plans." I try to smile, hoping it seems normal from the outside. Cassie will be at Emmett's tonight, since they're dating, so I knew I'd have the place to myself. I thought maybe Tyler could stay at my house for once, or it'd at least be easier for me to sneak over to his. Does it even count as sneaking if Cassie is hardly home anyway? She's in the apartment less than I am these days, so it's a miracle when we happen to be there at the same time.

But instead of hanging out with Tyler, I'm going home alone tonight.

And I'm more confused than ever.

Two hours later and I'm home, sitting on the couch doom-scrolling to avoid thinking about Tyler.

I jump when loud knocks come from the other side of the front door, followed by the voice of the person I'm trying hard not to think about.

"Lucy, let me in."

Here come the tears.

"Lucy, please."

My body is frozen to the couch, but my feet want to move, to walk over to the door, to let him in. My thoughts are conflicting with my heart, and even though I *want* more than anything to envelop him in a hug, I can't.

"Lucy, I'm sorry." A loud thump echoes through the door, and I can assume his head is slumped against it. "Please. I know I messed up, okay? Can we talk?"

I close my eyes, let out a long sigh, then finally move to stand up and let him in.

I twist the lock and open the door, then walk back to the couch. Tyler enters the room, closing the door behind him. This is his first time inside, but he doesn't spend time perusing my belongings like I did my first time at his place.

Instead, he's kneeling in front of me. He alternates between sighing and shaking his head as he rubs my knees. I've seen him have a panic attack before and can tell he's at the start of one now. He's grounding himself on me, breathing in a regular pattern to try and calm his heart. I ache for him, for what he's going through, but I can't erase my own pain.

The toil in my heart looms large as I sit and stare at him, wondering if I should pull him closer or push him away.

Ultimately, my heart wins and I pull him close to me, rubbing his back in a vertical motion.

"Shh," I whisper into his ear.

His breathing is quick against my body, so I keep shushing him. Trying to aid him in coming down from what he's going through.

He buries his head in my neck, and we stay like this for a few minutes.

I love him *so* much, and it hurts to see him like this. To know that there's nothing I can do to fix it but be patient and let him work through it. It pains me to know how often he's experienced this at varying degrees, that he hasn't had someone there for him.

Any other day I would sit here with him for hours, help him work through his attack. Except I'm hurting too. And because of that, I pull back once his breathing starts to slow.

"Lucy, pretty girl, look at me," he pleads.

I glance up from the floor to him. His face is red and splotchy, his eyes are glossy. Tears stain his cheeks and his eyelashes flutter as he blinks rapidly to keep more from falling.

My own tears start to fall, adding to my already puffy face, and his thumb is there to wipe them away.

"You weren't there," I mutter through struggling breaths.

"I know," he whispers, averting his eyes for a brief moment.

"You weren't there," I repeat. "Why?"

"I..." He trails off, his hand moving to my thigh to rub small circles. "I wanted to be. I had my keys in hand. I was putting on my shoes. And then I got a text from my mom. She was in town already. And so I went to see her, thinking I could be a few minutes late. But then my mom didn't even show up. And when I was driving to see you, I just...I couldn't. I just kept thinking, what if this isn't what I think it is? Which is erratic to think about because of how much you mean to me. I don't know what else to say..."

"This was an important moment, Tyler," I whisper.

"I know," he says, and it breaks my heart to know that he *chose* to not come tonight. He *chose* to go back home, even though he would have made it with more than enough time.

"I—I don't think I can do this right now," I admit.

"I know I fucked up, Lucy. Please don't do this," Tyler begs. He cups my face with both hands, trying to get me to look at him, but I shake out of his hold.

This is too much. I can't have this doubt in the back of my mind while I'm trying to secure my future, whatever that may be.

I can't be constantly wondering if he's going to be there, show up, when I really need him.

I gave him a chance even though I was done dating, done focusing on things other than my art. One chance, nothing more. At least, not right now.

"I need to focus on my showcase. I—" I stand up from the couch and pace in a line, crossing my arms over my body, hugging myself. "I just need time. And you need to figure out if I'm a priority. If I'm important enough to be there for."

"You *are*. You are important, Lucy. I wouldn't be here right now, begging for you to not do this if you weren't." Tyler comes up to me, trying to touch me, but I back away.

I shake my head and let the tears fall.

"I would have understood if you would have talked to me. Texted me. Told me why you couldn't be there. I would have come over after, or last night when you were already having thoughts about backing out."

"But I wasn't feeling this last night. Fuck. Lucy, I'm head over heels for you. I—" Tyler stalks forward, but I retreat, knowing that if he touches me, I'll fold.

"Tyler, please," I whisper, pleading with him to let me have time alone.

"Okay, okay." He walks backward to the door. He reaches for the handle, but before he leaves, he says my name, so I meet his stare. "I'm holding on. To this. To us. I'm going to give you time, but we aren't done. You hear me, pretty girl? This isn't something that's temporary."

I hold myself together until the door latches shut, then I crumble to the floor.

13
TYLER

One week.

That's how long it's been since I talked to Lucy.

Well, that's not true. I've talked to Lucy, texted her, but she hasn't responded.

Not that I expect her to, but when she asked for time I didn't know what to do besides say okay.

I had to text Emmett and ask him if he thinks we broke up, and then he asked me if I asked her. Obviously I didn't. I didn't know I was supposed to.

He was no help.

And so I'm here with Jon for an emergency session because I needed someone to talk to.

"You keep checking your phone," Jon notes, scribbling *something* into that notebook of his.

"Very perceptive," I snap. "Sorry, I didn't mean that."

"It's okay," Jon says.

"I tried to be there, to be what you call *emotionally available*." I add quotes around his term because it's clearly not working out for me.

"And how did that work out for you?"

Do therapists always ask this many questions? It's never straightforward advice, it's always some sort of question or vague metaphor for me to sort through later.

"I'm sitting here on your couch." I raise a brow. "We are broken up? Not broken up? I don't know, it's a gray area. I've been wanting to give her space, but I can't help but text her. I'm going insane. It's been a week. I see her car sitting outside the diner when I leave the studio. I've heard Cassie talking to her on the phone. And then there's my mom, who didn't apologize about not showing up but continues to text me as if nothing happened."

"Mhm, yes. I got that. So, you pushed Lucy away?" Jon asks, his pen hovering next to his face.

"No, I didn't push her away." I shake my head.

"You told her you wouldn't be at her event?"

"Well." I think for a moment. "No."

"And did you tell her that when your mom showed up it led you to feeling like you've been left all over again?"

"Well, no. I didn't exactly—"

"And did you tell her how you feel about her?" Jon interrupts.

These fucking questions.

"She knows enough, yes." I mean, mostly. She knows I like her. I've told her basically every day. "One can argue she's the one that pushed me away. She's the one that told me she needs time. Not me. I know what I want."

"Do you?" Jon asks, writing more in his notebook.

"I...yes. I, um, it's complicated, okay?" My temper rises as Jon settles with nodding while I speak. "Imagine you're me and you believe you're better off alone, that no one is worth the heartbreak, and anyone you get close to will leave. And then you meet someone who challenges that, challenges you, and you think...huh, maybe I'll try. Maybe I'll fucking try. And so you do, and you end up falling so fucking hard. It's like your heart is being hit by a never-ending fucking train, but it's calming, soothing even, to think about this person that you fucking love. But it's also a lot, so overwhelming that some of those thoughts trickle back in, and you realize how much you'll get hurt, so you back away a little, just enough to know if she feels the same way..." I stop talking.

I...

I pushed her away.

I love her.

I pushed her away.

14
LUCY

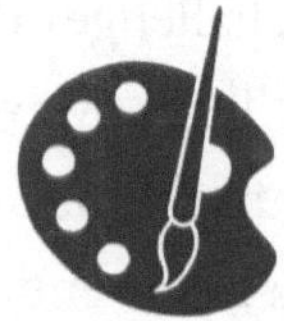

People underestimate how soothing a cup of tea and some classical music can be.

"Luce, what are you doing?" Cassie's voice comes from behind me.

I pause the music on my phone and spin around in the stool. I've been sitting in the kitchen for the past hour, thinking and trying not to think at the same time.

"N-nothing." I stumble over my words. "I'm fine."

"You're clearly not fine." Cassie walks into the kitchen, grabs a mug for herself from the pantry and pours a cup of coffee.

"I—"

My phone dings, the noise echoing around the room. I flinch. I forgot it was hooked to the speaker.

Cassie, unfortunately, sees my phone before I'm able to snag it.

"Fuck," I mumble under my breath.

"Um, Lucy, why is Tyler texting you and telling you that he's thinking about you?"

We only know one Tyler, so she already knows who he is without having to ask.

"Lucy, are you dating Tyler?" Cassie asks after I don't answer her first question.

"Kind of? Yes? I don't know. It's complicated." I grimace, knowing that she's probably upset from me not telling her when she's confided in me about Emmett.

"Explain please."

And so I do. I tell her everything while she sits there and listens. She tries to chime in every other sentence to ask a clarifying question, but I keep talking. She does that, likes to interrupt when she gets excited or invested in something.

"So, you told him *you* need time?"

"Yeah, I did."

Cassie hums.

"What?" I ask. "Just say it."

"Oh, nothing, just can't believe you fell in love with someone and I wasn't around to notice."

"I didn't fall in love with someone." I try to argue, but it's weak. My tone is barely above whisper, and Cassie knows me better than that. "Okay, fine, I love Tyler."

"Mhm." Cassie smiles, happy with herself for getting the truth out of me. "So remind me why you aren't talking to him? Shit, Luce, he's texted you every day for the last two weeks. And oh, that's a picture..."

I rip the phone from her hands. She's lucky she stumbled on that picture; it's tame compared to some of the others I've since deleted. He at least kept his pants on in that one.

"I just need to focus on my paintings. I have a month until my showcase, and if I don't get my art to be a cohesive unit, then I'm done with it for good."

"You couldn't be done with art, Luce," Cassie says.

And she has a point, I couldn't.

"No, but like you, I was never going to work at this diner for long. I was supposed to have found a gallery space already. And I'm giving this one last go before I force myself to decide what's next for me. So I didn't want to worry about whether or not Tyler would be there for me, I didn't want those thoughts nagging at me when I still am trying to finalize my pieces."

"And what if he's not there when you finally decide that you're ready?" Cassie says.

If after the showcase, he decides he doesn't want me, then… I guess that'll be that.

After talking to Cassie, I spend the rest of the afternoon in the studio, trying to get the pieces right for the showcase.

Tyler texts me again, but I ignore it.

I channel all energy into these canvases, throwing blues and pinks at it to see what sticks. When I showed Tyler my previous paintings, they were *almost* there. There are still a few tweaks I want to make to ensure that everything is perfect. I have a few weeks until the showcase. A few weeks until my career is either set for the near future, or it's time to maybe try to pursue it part-time instead.

Time passes slowly as I work through multiple canvases. Each one turns out worse than the one before.

"Fuck," I say to myself.

I slump in the middle of the room and sob.

This break is supposed to be good. Tyler's giving me time, but he's still there. Every text is a reminder that he's still there.

My phone dings. Again. The universe must have told him I was thinking about him.

Tyler

> When you're ready, I'll be here.

And when I wake up the next morning, I grab my phone, expecting to see another text from him.

Except there's nothing.

For the first time in two weeks, there's no unread message from him. His normal 'have a good day, pretty girl' isn't in my inbox.

And instead of sobbing into my pillow, like I want to do I force myself to get up, to get dressed, and create three damn good art pieces because if I don't get a spot at the gallery, then this spout of heartbreak was for nothing.

15
TYLER

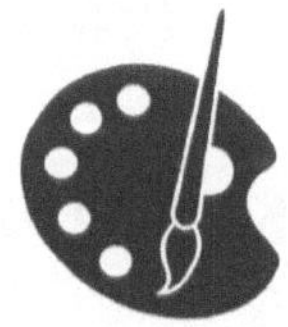

I'm sitting in my apartment as the walls start to close in. They crumble, but I can't move.

No matter how hard I try to stand up, I can't move. I look down and see that my lower body is shackled to the floor. I scream, but no one hears me. There's no one.

No one.

Blackness overtakes my vision, and then I sit up.

It was just a dream.

A nightmare.

My breathing is ragged as I sink my head into my hands.

It's been a month since I've seen Lucy.

A month since I've heard her laugh.

I stopped texting her two weeks ago, thinking that maybe she would text me.

I waited.

There were moments where I'd check our text thread and at the same time would see the bubbles pop up, a signal that she was thinking of texting me. But then they disappeared and nothing followed. At least she was thinking of me enough to type something out, even if she did erase it in the end.

I have an hour until I need to meet Emmett for breakfast. He and the others have been trying to drag me from my place when we aren't working, trying to keep me company. I let them, but we don't talk about Lucy. They tried the first week, when they saw how irritable I was, but stopped bringing it up when I finally told them I wouldn't hang out with them if they wouldn't drop it.

I rummage around the apartment, cleaning an already-clean room. It's the one thing that keeps my mind occupied and helps keep me from thinking about Lucy. It's impossible to forget her while I exist in the space she occupied for the duration of our relationship, remembering the nights she stayed over, noticing her smell still lingering on anything fabric. Would it be too much to ask for my mind to temporarily *not* think about her? To put me out of my misery?

Apparently.

Cleaning keeps me busy until it's time to go to meet Emmett for breakfast. We are going to Flora Coffee, a place that sells our favorite muffins, to avoid seeing Lucy if she happens to be working at the diner. I know she doesn't typically work in the mornings, since that's usually the time when she paints, but I didn't want to risk it. I also didn't want Emmett to ask Cassie, because I didn't want Lucy to get word of it. I'm *trying* to give her space, for real this time.

Emmett and I both order a blueberry muffin and black coffee and then take a seat in a booth.

"Have you heard from your mom recently?" Emmett asks, pouring two sugars into his coffee.

I shake my head. "No. Although I don't expect to. I texted her and made sure she knew I didn't have money for her. I figured that's why she wanted to come see me anyhow, so I might as well tell her so she can decide if it's worth coming or not. Clearly she doesn't want to see her son, she just wants the money." I shrug.

I've come to terms with my mom, that she just isn't the person I wanted her to be. But I've learned to be okay with it because I have my own chosen family. Emmett, Max, Lane, Marcy — they have been there for me. And now Cassie, and maybe Lucy... they are all who I would rather spend time with.

"Sorry, Tyler."

"Eh, it's fine. I kind of expected it. It's not the worst thing that's happened to me recently." I huff a laugh.

"You know she asked how you were..." Emmett doesn't look at me when he speaks because he knows the rule. No talking about Lucy. But does he listen? No.

"Why are you telling me this?"

"Maybe you should reach out to her."

I shake my head and take a bite of my muffin. "She said she wanted time."

"You gave her time, and you both are clearly miserable."

"She needs to come to me. I told her I'd be here if she needs me, but I don't want to push my luck. I don't want to try again, only to have her reject me all together. If there's even a chance she wants me, I don't want to screw it up."

"Don't tell me you're not going to go to her showcase," Emmett says.

"I don't know if she wants me there."

"Everyone is going."

"I'm not everyone, Em. I don't want to add more stress to her night, not when she told me she needs to focus."

If she wanted me there, she would tell me, right? Or am I supposed to assume that she wants me there? This is all confusing, and she knows that I'm not used to having a partner in life. Not like this, not someone that relies on you and expects you to be there even when they don't ask.

And I would have been. I would have been there if we weren't taking a break or whatever the fuck this is. A temporary breakup. I would have been there.

"But this showcase feels kind of important, doesn't it?" Emmett asks, his mouth full of muffin.

"What did you say?" I jerk my head toward him.

"This showcase feels kind of important?" Emmett raises his brows and looks at me like *what is wrong with you*.

This showcase is important.

It's an important moment.

And the way you show someone you care is to be there for the important moments.

They're the ones that matter.

I slam my hand down on the table, finally knowing what to do to win her back.

Hopefully.

16
LUCY

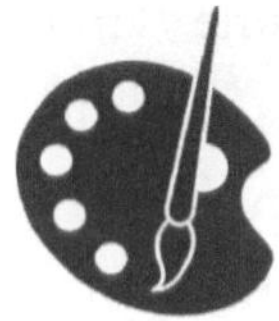

THE PIECES ARE DONE. In addition to the three main pieces that I've been working on, the ones that will make the most impact, I've painted ten additional smaller ones that are related in style. I also made some prints in case someone wants something of mine but can't afford the large paintings.

This spot at the gallery is mine; it has to be. If it goes to someone else, I'll have to wait until there is another vacancy.

And since it's downtown Los Angeles, gallery spaces can be far and few between.

The truck is here to cart my work over, so after I load everything and triple check that nothing will fall over, I give the driver a nod that it's good. Once it gets to the venue, they have staff who know what to do.

That eases my nerves.

A little bit.

I shake out my hands as I go back inside to where Cassie is pacing around the room. She's still getting used to being public with Emmett. A month ago they went on live television to announce that Emmett was done with acting and that he and Cassie were an item.

Since then, she's had to learn to adjust to being more in the spotlight than ever. Between this and her role in a new movie, her anxiety is about the same as mine about this showcase.

"You all good?" she asks as I enter the room.

"Hm? Oh, yeah, I mean... fine I suppose." I rub the side of my arm and look around the room. If everything works out... *when* everything works out, this will no longer be my studio.

There's paint everywhere, in cans and jars, but also on the floor and the ceiling and the walls. There are over four years of memories here, of paintings that I've done, of the emotions I've worked through. Painting is, and always will be, my safe space.

It's the one constant in my life. Well, besides Cassie, but she doesn't count. Painting is like breathing. It's natural. Without it, I don't think I'd survive.

"Have you heard from *you know who*?" Cassie teases me with a spooky tone.

I shake my head. Tyler hasn't texted me in a month. Cassie refuses to tell me anything that's been happening with him. She won't tell me if he looks happy or if he looks the opposite. She won't tell me if he's asked about me, or if he's asked Emmett. I suppose that's good, that she won't tell me anything, if she knows anything at all.

The one thing she did say is that she hasn't seen him a lot, that apparently he doesn't leave his office very much while at work and then retreats back to his place every night. I frequently thought about how easy it'd be to call or text him. Maybe I'd just drop by his place, knock on his door and demand to be let in like he did to me.

Except I wouldn't have to demand.

I doubt I'd have to knock twice.

He'd be there, ready for me, and that terrifies me.

It's ironic that he was the one that didn't seem ready for a relationship. He was the one still dealing with his own shit. And here I am, being the stubborn one and not talking to him. But I have reasons, like the importance of this showcase and the constant worry I would have had to endure if he missed another important moment.

But here I am anyway, wondering if he will be at the gallery tonight.

"Is it time?" Cassie pulls her phone out of her pocket to check. "Oh, yes, we need to leave now. Um, I'll call the car around? I guess? God, that feels so weird to say."

"You're famous now, Cass." I shrug. "Better get used to it."

"I landed one role, Luce. It's not like I'm an A-list actor or anything."

"You are dating one, though. I think that adds to your level of fame."

She groans and throws an arm over my shoulder as we walk toward the door. "Oh shush, it does not. Emmett may have written the script and asked me to be the lead, but I don't know if I'll land more roles after this. For now, I'm just grateful for the one. Can you try to talk to Tyler the next time you see him?"

"You said his name." I glare at her.

"Oh, shit," she says, covering her mouth with her free hand. "I mean, *you know who*. You'll talk to him. Or at least think about calling him after tonight. You deserve to be happy, and this will be the only time I'll say it... I don't want you to murder me in my sleep... but he makes you happy."

I inhale a large amount of air and nod, then exhale and mumble, "I promise, okay?"

"Good. Now, let's go sell some art."

An hour later, we are finally at the gallery. *Thank you rush hour.*

Luckily, Cassie planned for this. We left the studio early and had some time to kill once we got there since my art was already set up. Just one final walk through to confirm everything is where I mapped it out to be, and we are ready to go.

It's nearly six p.m. when the crowd arrives.

One by one, various people filter by. Mostly couples, or groups of friends, walk by and strike up conversations. They whisper to each other, and I try to overhear what they are saying. I only catch snippets.

"This art is beautiful, isn't it?"

"Oh, wow. Is that the sky? It's so abstract, but in a good way."

"I love how these go together so effortlessly."

"Absolutely breathtaking."

I'm grinning ear to ear the entire time, my mind hardly wandering to *you know who*. Except now. I'm most definitely wishing he was here to witness the kind words that these random strangers have to say about the art that I spent many, many, many hours trying to get right. I'm looking around the room to see if I see anyone I know when I overhear a couple say, *"Too bad all of these pieces have been bought. I would have loved to buy one for my house."*

"Um, excuse me," I say to the couple. "Did you say that all my paintings were bought?"

The shock is settling in, and it's hard to tell if they are playing a prank on me. Are there cameras I don't know about? I glance around the room again, quickly, to confirm the whole no camera thing, then look at them.

They simply nod, like *duh*, and say, "Oh, yes. Congratulations, we love your work. Could we have your contact information? I'd love to inquire about a custom piece."

"Uh—Oh—Um—" I stumble, but Cassie slides up next to me at the perfect moment.

"Here's her card, she'd love that." Cassie hands them a business card and I mouth *thanks* to her.

"Great, we will be in contact. It was great meeting you, Lucy. I'll make sure to put in a good word to the owner of the gallery. He's a close friend of mine," the random stranger says and then disappears through the crowd.

"Lucy! You lucky goose. Did I just overhear her say that all your art has been bought?" Cassie asks.

I spin around in a circle to face my art, glancing at all the price tags.

"Uh, yeah, um... I think I need a moment, Cass. Can you watch my work for me? I'm going to take a lap around the room."

"Yeah, of course, happy to." Cassie smiles, which helps ease the shock a little.

I just nod and take deep breaths, then I walk to the right. In addition to a few people trying to get permanent spots, there are some residents here that I want to check out.

There's someone who only paints in monochrome. They do all sorts of portraits, and it's incredible.

There's another person that does watercolor paintings of historical events, but they add flowers to any sort of weapon.

And then there's my favorite, another abstract artist, but they paint darker themes. I find myself being drawn to their art the most, because it always resonates with my internal feelings.

I walk and mingle for a moment, feeling the knot loosen in my chest with each conversation.

And I wish it could loosen more, until it's no longer a knot, but strings that can be strummed.

I'm not watching where I'm going when I turn the corner and bump into a hard chest.

"Oh, um, I'm sorry. I wasn't watching where—" I look up and my words are cut off. My mind blank. My palms sweat.

"Hi, pretty girl," the man in front of me whispers.

Tyler is standing in front of me.

He's wearing a suit.

Tyler is standing in front of me.

I turn around and start to walk toward the bathroom on the other side of the venue. It's a straight walk, twenty or thirty steps and I'd be there. I just need to keep walking straight.

My plan was going great until I remembered the giant sculpture artist and they happened to be carting a twenty-foot statue of something that stops me in my tracks.

"Wait, don't go," a voice whispers in my ear as two strong hands clasp either arm.

A hand applies pressure to my back as Tyler takes a step forward to close the distance.

"You look beautiful tonight," he says as he trails a hand down my arm.

My head leans back ever so slightly without my permission.

I miss him.

So much.

I miss him the way I miss when I can't paint.

What am I even doing anymore?

Why am I fighting *this*? Clearly I don't want to.

He's here, for this, for this important moment.

"A very smart and beautiful woman once told me that it was the important moments that counted. And even though I listened, I missed an important moment. I knew I should have been there, and yet I wasn't there. And because of that, the small foundation of trust that I built with this woman crumbled, and I wanted more than anything to rebuild it. And so I tried." Tyler takes a deep breath. He continues to talk to me in the middle of this gallery, continues to whisper into my ear so no one else can hear. "I tried, but I didn't try hard enough."

I turn around then, a tear falling down my cheek. His thumb is right there to sweep it away.

"You did try hard enough. I was the stubborn one," I whisper.

"No, pretty girl, you needed me and I wasn't there. But I'm here now."

"You're here now," I say, tucking my bottom lip between my teeth.

"And there's this question I've been wanting to ask you ever since I saw you from across the room."

"Oh, really?" I chuckle, feeling happy that he's here and overwhelmed with where this might be going. If he wants me back, or I guess doesn't want to officially break up, I already know what I'm going to say.

"Yep." He nods. "I've heard from some very close sources that you don't date. Is that accurate?"

"Is that your question?"

"Please answer the question, pretty girl."

I refrain from rolling my eyes and play his game, except it's my turn. "That is correct. But there *is* this man that I love, and I've been waiting for the right moment to tell him. Do you have any advice?"

"Uh." He coughs and his eyes widen as if he's trying to figure out if I'm messing with him or if this is all real. "Do you think this man loves you back?"

"Great question. All signs point to yes, but I haven't seen him in a while. And well, I was waiting for him to ask me on a date again, so that I could tell him in person."

"Well, I'm positive the answer is yes, but while you wait for him, would you mind if I asked you another question?"

I hum for a moment. "Might as well, who knows how long he will keep me waiting."

"Will you go on a date with me? Just one date. You and me." Tyler's arms wrap tighter around my waist and I don't care one bit that we are in an event space full of a hundred people.

In this moment, it's just us.

"One date? That's all you want?" I ask.

Tyler nods, his smile widening into a grin. "I thought about asking for a lifetime, but figure I'd save that for another day."

"One date. Let's see if you can leave me feeling a little bit inspired."

17

EPILOGUE: TYLER

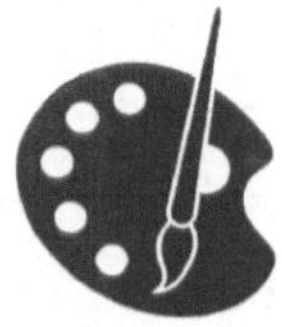

ONE WEEK LATER

"Where are you taking me?" Lucy looks over at me from the passenger seat of my car. It's the middle of the day in November, and the weather is perfect.

"Just wait, Luce. If you'd stop asking me, we might be there already," I tease.

"Oh, shush. That's not how it works."

I glance over at her for a brief moment in time to see her shake her head and smile to herself.

"We are almost there, okay?" My hand finds her leg and I squeeze before she brings her hand over mine, interlacing our fingers.

"Okay," she drawls and turns up the radio to continue singing to some random pop song I only know the melody of.

I have to bite my lip to stop myself from smiling, from laughing, from saying something dumb. She's not a bad singer, it's not that. It's just *her*. Her hair flowing in the breeze from the window, the tapping from her fingers on my hand to the beat of the song, and the effortless way she sings even when she doesn't know all the words.

One week later, and I'm still kicking myself for almost missing out on this, on us. I like to think that things would have worked out eventually, timing would have been on our side, things would have been different. But I would have lost that time, and I'm glad I had the idea to show up at her showcase.

And buy all her art.

I did that too.

I plan to display some of it in my apartment, and I've already gifted a few pieces to people that I've met from January Studios; people that will buy more and spread the word about her talent.

She doesn't know that though, not yet. Although, she will soon, hopefully, if she says yes to the question I'll be asking her shortly.

I turn on the familiar gravel road, but with how loud Lucy has the music turned up, you would never know if you couldn't see where we were headed.

Lucky for us, the sun shines and the trees are shades of auburn and brown and orange and yellow. The surroundings are helping the ever growing ache in my chest around the possibility that she might say no.

I hope she doesn't.

"Tyler, it's our spot." Lucy beams as I park in front of the field of wildflowers. There may not be anything blooming at the moment, but that doesn't take away from the scenery. Instead, the wispy brown and dark green flora that add to it.

"I thought it'd be a perfect place for what I had planned." I smile and hop out of the car before she can ask me what we're doing.

The trunk has everything I need, and I'm thankful that it's all packed neatly (I hope) into a giant box.

Lucy rounds the back and gives me a weary look. "Just a reminder, Cassie has my location."

"Oh, shush, pretty girl. Grab these towels, please."

"Not helping your case. Towels, a giant box, a remote location..." Lucy counts each reason on a finger.

"You know," I walk to set the box down at the edge of the field, then go back to her, "there are other things that require a remote location. Maybe you should open the box."

"Is this some sort of sex thing? The ground is wet and it's too cold, Ty—"

"Lucy, just open the box."

"Fine, fine," she grumbles. When she reaches the box, she looks back over her shoulder at me one last time and I give her a nod to continue. "Okay, here goes nothing..."

She grabs the flaps of the box and opens them, one by one.

"Tyler..." she whispers and starts to remove the contents.

Two canvases, paint, and brushes.

"I figured since we cooked together, it was time for us to paint together." I walk over and grab the box from Lucy, moving it out of my way so I can step in front of her and pull her into a hug.

"And at this spot?" She leans her head back to look at me.

I tuck a strand of hair behind her ear and press my lips against hers, soft and slow.

"Yes." I pull back. "Our first date was here, and I'm pretty sure it's where I started to fall in love with you."

"That early, huh?" Lucy teases. I pinch her side in return, causing us both to start laughing.

She lays her head on my chest, her breathing syncing with mine as we become silent and the only sounds around us are the chirping of birds and the crunching of leaves.

"Well," Lucy mutters, "I wouldn't have said yes in the first place if I didn't feel something different about you. So, I guess you can say I have you beat."

"Well, shit, pretty girl, who knew you were so obsessed with me from the beginning."

She tries to push me away, but I grab her tighter and squeeze until she does it back.

"I love you," I whisper and kiss her temple.

"I love you, too," she says and lifts her head off me to give me a kiss. "Ready to paint?"

"I, um, have a question to ask you first."

Lucy's eyes narrow and she purses her lips. "Tyler...what are you..."

I let go of her and take a step back, lowering to one knee.

The box in my left pant pocket has been weighing me down all day, and I was nervous she'd see or feel it.

I pull it out, holding the velvet box in front of me as Lucy continues to be shocked.

"Lucy, I love you. My whole life, I've felt like I had to search for love, or better yet, I had to search for ways to keep love around. And when that became too difficult, I thought I'd be better off without it. I shut myself off, let some new version of myself take over, and figured I was happy with that.

"But then I met you. And I was so nervous to talk to you because I could tell something was different from the first time our eyes met. You made me laugh, and I felt like the luckiest guy in the room that you were sitting with me.

"The more I've gotten to know you, the more I love you. And the more I love you, the more I want to be around you every hour of every day. So, Lucy…"

I open the velvet box with a rose gold key to my apartment inside.

"Will you move in with me?"

Lucy doesn't say anything for a moment, but her cheeks are stained with tears from what I just confessed.

"I don't know if I should kiss you or kill you right now."

"Is that a yes, pretty girl?"

Lucy reaches for the key and pockets it. "Yes, and it's good timing too with Cassie moving out. I was going to need to look for a new place to stay."

I hold her hand as I stand up, pulling her into my arms. "You are forever welcome at my place," I mumble into her hair.

Little does she know, I have a ring waiting for her back at the apartment, but I'm waiting for a really special day to give that to her. She deserves the world, and I'm going to try to give her a small piece of it every day.

I pull back enough to press a kiss to her forehead and say, "Okay, let's paint."

Acknowledgements

I wrote this story as a way to challenge myself. Lucy and Tyler were always "together" in my head. I wasn't sure if I wanted to tell their story. But thanks to close friends (and readers), I decided to write this novella.

And to be honest, I *think* Lucy and Tyler are my favorite couple to date.

I put a lot of myself in Tyler, having been diagnosed with panic attacks earlier in the year. Life has gotten better since being able to put a name to the feelings I experience.

Now, for the thank yous!

I want to thank Kristen, Sophie, and the rest of the Indy Writing Coven. You all keep me motivated!

I want to thank Beth for loving my characters as much as me and being the best editor. (And sorry if there are typos in this because I wrote it last minute!!!!!!!!)

To my alpha and beta readers, thank you for giving me lots of wonderful notes and feedback.

And to my husband Ryan, for constantly listening to me rave about these characters that live inside my head. Love you forever!

About the Author

Courtney Corlew lives in the Midwest with her husband Ryan and their two kids. When she's not writing, she's reading (like everyone else) and spending time in coffee shops and bookstores around the city. She looks forward to writing many more stories filled with dreams, love, and friendship. To stay up to date, follow her on Instagram @courtneycorlewauthor or visit her website www.courtneycorlewauthor.com.